BLUE MOONLIGHT

Published by Thomas & Mercer
P.O. Box 400818
Las Vegas, NV 89140

ISBN-13: 9781612183428
ISBN-10: 1612183425

BLUE MOONLIGHT

A DICK MOONLIGHT THRILLER

VINCENT ZANDRI

fTHOMAS & MERCER

This bitter earth can be so cold.
—Will Grosz

For Laura

PART I

CHAPTER 1

I'm awake.

I know I'm awake because my eyes are open and I'm looking down at my hands, which are handcuffed. Funny how I don't remember going to sleep in the first place.

Turns out I don't remember boarding a plane either.

But I know I'm on a plane because when I shift my focus from my handcuffed hands to over my left shoulder and out the window, I see nothing but friendly blue sky resting atop an endless sea of the fluffiest white cotton-ball clouds you ever did see.

For sure I'm flying.

I. Am. Flying.

Thirty thousand feet above solid ground, inside what looks to be an Airbus. A US Airways–owned and –operated Airbus. Or so says the color-coded, impervious-to-puncture/sudden-impact/water-and/or-fire-damage, floatable, plastic-coated safety manual stuffed inside the conveniently located seatback pocket directly in front of me.

Or maybe I'm just dreaming.

Tell you what. I'm gonna close my eyes now. Go back to sleep. Wake up in my own bed.

CHAPTER 2

I open my eyes.

Wide.

Still flying. Not lying in my own bed. Not imagining things. Not dreaming.

Fuck me.

CHAPTER 3

Recap thus far.

I'm awake. I'm handcuffed. I'm flying. And it isn't a dream.

Far as I can tell, I'm seated in the final row of the plane. The *bouncy-bouncy* seat, as my ex-wife, Lynn, used to call it whenever we'd take a trip together, which wasn't very often.

The cheap seat.

At first glance, there appear to be no seat assignments in the final rows of this plane. But that's not exactly right, because the seat directly beside my own has most definitely been assigned. To say the guy occupying it is bigger than me would be like saying the Super Bowl is just another meaningless pro football game.

Dude's so big he fills the narrow seat entirely, some of his excess bulk oozing over onto me. I'm not talking fat blubber here. I'm talking sheer, thick, hard muscle mass. The hand that's attached to the wrist to which my right wrist is cuffed is bigger and thicker than both my hands put together. And I'm no lightweight. I'm a weight lifter. I can bench press two hundred and sixty-five pounds ten, sometimes fifteen times in a row. Clean. None of this bouncing it off your chest cavity shit like all the high school meatheads do. But this Sherman tank of a man makes me feel about as rough and tumble as your average hopeless anorexic.

Like I already said, the half dozen rows of seats up ahead of me are unoccupied, as are the starboard rows to my right. A thick gray curtain is draped across the entire midsection of the cabin, as if to afford me the utmost privacy. Or it could be that the back rows have been closed off to the general law-abiding public due to my presence. But I can't imagine why in the world that could be.

I'm not a criminal.

My name is Dick Moonlight, and I'm just a head case who barely survives on a cop's half pension and the occasional private dick job I can scrounge up. A suicide survivor who carries a small piece of .22 caliber hollow-point lodged inside his brain. By all rights, I should be a dead man. But then there's not a whole lot of right surrounding me these days since my girlfriend left me for another man, since my sweet, bushy-haired little boy, Harrison, went to live with his mother in LA and at the same time ripped the pumping heart out of my chest, since my bar—Moonlight's Moonlit Manor—burned to the ground, since Jack Daniels came back into my life in a big way.

Welcome to my world.

The plane dips and lifts and dips again, the entire fuselage rattling and shaking. An overhead light clicks on, along with a gentle chime.

PLEASE FASTEN YOUR SEAT BELTS.

You ain't gotta tell me twice.
But then, I'm already strapped in.

A tinny voice emerges over the PA asking us fliers to return to our seats and fasten our seat belts until the captain decides to turn off the warning light or we crash. Whichever comes first. We're about to encounter a patch of severe headwind-instigated turbulence that simply cannot be avoided.

Severe. Turbulence.

It rings a bell. No, it more than rings a bell. Just the sound of those two words sends my balls on a vertical rise up through my colon, through my stomach, and on up into my throat, where they settle like two concrete lumps.

I tap into my memory banks. What's left of them.

I'm flying.

But I don't like to fly.

I hate flying.

I'm afraid to fly.

No, that's not right.

I'm afraid of crashing.

We hit the promised patch of turbulence.

The plane rocks like a boat on a choppy sea. A wave of cold fear rushes through my body. But the big guy next to me, he's smiling.

Correction.

He's laughing. Laughing like flying through severe turbulence is the most fun you can have with and without your clothes on. What's even worse is that every time we hit a wave of bad air, he yanks on the cuffs, the sharp end of the bracket digging into my wrist as if going for bone. I'm beginning to think he's drawing blood.

"Mister," I say, my voice a full octave higher than the good Lord intended. "Mister. Sir. Mister."

He turns to me. He's sporting this big-ass smile that's centered in a bowling-ball-round face, thick red lips surrounded by a goatee and mustache that's far thicker than my own. His hair is thick too, but sprinkled with gray and balding in the middle. I peg him for maybe fifty, but going on sixteen. You know the type.

"Well look who's awake!" he barks. "And just in time too. We're in for a ride. Turbulence. Makes things interesting, don't you think? My three marriages were chock-full of turbulence. Never a dull day, sweetie."

Sweetie…? Did this bruiser just call me sweetie?

He laughs, shaking his belly, which protrudes up tight against a Hawaiian print shirt that must have been specially woven for one of those huge-ass Samoan motherfuckers. He's opening and closing the fingers on his left hand, the middle digit of which bears a thick gold ring with a big red gemstone embedded inside it. The stone is bigger than my eye, and I'm betting the entire thing must weigh in at five pounds. Even from where I'm sitting, I can see the letters NFL embossed into the gold band.

Football.

Pro football.

I love football.

But this guy's a dick.

Situation check.

I'm flying.

I'm handcuffed to a bigger-than-big man who enjoys turbulence. Handcuffed to a big man who likes turbulence and who used to play pro ball, and who just referred to me as sweetie. Attached at the wrist to an NFL man and flying through some of the worst turbulence I've ever experienced and I have no idea how I got myself into this little predicament.

Which, of course, begs the question...

"How did I get here?"

"You mean, like...here?" NFL Man says, yanking on the cuffs, sending a wave of electric pain shooting up my right arm. "Oops, my bad. You mean *here* on this plane? You tell me, sweetie...What's your name again?" Reaching into his shirt pocket and pulling out a slip of yellow Post-it note. "Mr. Richard Moonlight, date of birth seven-two-sixty-something; Social Security number: zero-five-zero, yadda, yadda; height: five feet nine inches, even if you do look like five-seven with your boots on; weight: one hundred seventy-six pounds. Divorced, father of one poor unlucky kid, currently single after a crap load of fucked-up relationships. Or should I say, relationship fuck-ups." Staring down at me like I'm a booger on the armrest. "Five-seven and a buck seventy-six. Little guy, you are."

"I'm five-eight-and-a-half. And your scale must be off...I'm one-seventy." I wanna bust his ass for talking like Yoda, but I'm afraid he'll yank on that cuff chain again. And besides, the plane is bouncing and I'm too scared out of my skin for idle chatter.

Another jolt of turbulence. I feel my heart stop for the briefest of seconds. It starts up again.

"We get the info from the computer," he says and laughs. "We don't actually weigh you. And besides, you wouldn't have let us if we'd wanted to, anyway. Not in the condition you were in."

"What. Condition."

NFL Man just looks at me, into my eyes. "You don't remember, do you? You truly don't remember?"

"My head," I attempt to explain. "I have this problem with my brain. There's a—"

"Little piece of .22 caliber bullet inside it, pressed up against your cerebral cortex. Yes, yes, yes, I know all about it. You wouldn't shut up about it on the drive all the way to the airport."

"What drive?"

"From your crib to the airport. Plane didn't very well pick us up in front of your loft, Moonlight." Another belly laugh.

"OK, I give up. Who are you?"

Reaching back into his chest pocket, this time pulling out a wallet. When he does it, his unbuttoned shirt opens up enough to reveal a hand cannon stuffed inside a black elastic-banded shoulder holster.

Guns on a plane. Cop on a plane. Or hijacker on a plane.

I'm putting my money on the cop. If I had any money. Even I'm not lucky enough to be hijacked by a hijacker.

He opens the wallet, revealing a laminated picture ID. There he is, all smiles and wavy black hair that isn't yet sprinkled with gray. Big guy's got to get a new pic. I try to catch the name printed in between the photo and the letters *F, B,* and *I,* but only catch the last name.

Zumbo.

Now if that doesn't sound like a pro ball player, I don't know what does. Turns out I recognize the name.

Zumbo.

Bob "Zump" Zumbo, fullback for the New York Giants from 1987 through 1994 when a knee injury sidelined him for good.

I might be flying, on the verge of crashing, but things are definitely looking up. "Giants," I say.

Now the smile is so wide I fear it might split his entire face in half. "You a fan, Moonlight?"

I nod. "Never miss a game," I tell him. "You were pretty great. The return of Larry Csonka. The *Zonk*."

"Bad knees," he says, cocking his head down toward his lap. "I had to retire with half pension."

"That why you're a fed agent now?"

"The FBI is my hobby. Keeps me out of the bars."

"Mr., or is it Agent, Zumbo? Listen, I gotta pee something fierce. My back teeth are floating."

He purses his lips. "Ah jeez, really?" he says, annoyed. Like I'm his five-year-old kid. "OK, but you gotta make it quick. Lots of turbulence. Case your injured brain hasn't picked up on it."

Reaching into his pocket, he pulls out a key, uncuffs my wrist.

I feel immediate relief. The skin isn't broken, but it's scratched. I run the fingers of my left hand over it.

Zumbo pushes himself out of the seat, stands up, and shifts himself into the aisle. His body fills out the entire back end of the plane. "OK, Moonlight, up and at 'em. And don't try anything funny. We're on a commercial flight and I have a gun, and by the looks of things, you don't need any more trouble added to what's sure to be an impressive rap sheet.

Behind him, a female flight attendant approaches. "Do you think it's wise taking his cuffs off, Agent Zumbo?" she poses. She's a small but attractive redhead with long, smooth hair parted neatly over her right eye.

The plane buffets and rocks again, enough that Zumbo has to grab the seatback to stay on his feet. Meanwhile, the flight attendant seems entirely unaffected by the sudden motion. She's got her sea legs.

"Terrorists gotta pee too," he says and laughs, a little under his breath. "Constitution grants the right for a suspected criminal to water his teensy-weensy hog."

Back-stepping, the attractive redhead shakes her head in disgust and retreats into the aft galley. I know what she's thinking: *Men!*

Zumbo picks me up by the arm, leads me the two or three feet around to the emergency exit area behind our seats, where the lavatory is located. He opens the door and shoves me inside.

"One minute, sweetie," he insists. "Or I come in after you, guns a-blazin'."

"Yeah, I got it."

He goes to shut the door.

"Wait one second," I say. "What did you just refer to me as?"

The look on his round face has gone from glee to confusion. "Oh. Sweetie?" he barks. "I call lotsa people sweetie. Come on, Moonlight. Pee already."

"No, not that. I mean just a second ago when you were talking with the attendant. You called me something."

Back with the smile. "Oh, yeah. I called you a terrorist. Well, allow me to rephrase. You are *suspected* of performing a quote, 'domestic terroristic act,' unquote, to be accurate. You haven't been arrested for anything quite yet. You're merely being detained under suspicious circumstances. Think of it as being waitlisted for a spot in a federal pen."

"So where are we going and why have I been handcuffed and why does it take an airplane to get me there?"

"We're on our way to the Manhattan field office, for an interview."

"I don't understand. I'm not a terrorist. In fact, I used to be a cop."

"Hey, man," he says and exhales, "a Mrs. Doris E. Walsh of the Internal Revenue Service of these here United States of America disagrees entirely. And she can prove it." Pulling out a folded sheet of stock from the back pocket on his husky-size Levi's 501s. Unfolding it, he glances at it, then back at me. "Where'd you learn to construct pipe bombs, Moonlight?"

He shoves me farther into the bathroom, closes the door behind me. "One minute," he repeats from outside the door.

The plane shakes again. Dips. We're going down. I just know it. I'm gonna crash, burn, and die a tragic, violent death. Be identified later by my dental records.

But then that would be the best news I've heard all day.

CHAPTER 4

I turn, stare at the closed door.

The lock.

There's a small, door-mounted diagram telling me that if I should wish to engage the lock and the interior bathroom lights, I must slide the device to the left. At the same time, this will alert other passengers whose teeth are floating that this lavatory is presently "occupied." Zumbo didn't tell me not to engage the lock. It's one of those silent givens of the business, I'm sure. Which is why I reach up and slide the lock in place.

Moonlight the shifty.

The red light embedded into the small plastic laminate counter shines on.

OCCUPIED

A fist pounds on the door.

"Unlock that door, Moonlight!" Zumbo barks. "Or I'll put my fist through it and do it for you."

I'm still staring at the now-locked door. Still feeling the plane going bouncy-bounce under my feet.

Time to think. Quick. Me, the head case.

"Cut me some slack, agent!" I shout into the door. "I can't pee unless I know the door is locked. Stage fright. You know what that's like, right?"

I picture him standing naked inside a ceramic-covered locker room bathroom along with fifty other like-sized men, all of them naked, slapping each other's pale bare asses with white towels twisted into whips. In my head I hear him calling them "sweetie." I'm here to pee. I try to erase the thought from my memory.

But first I run the water, place my hands under the flow. I splash the cold water on my face, stare into the mirror.

Bloodshot eyes, sunk deep into black pools. Crow's-feet dug into the skin along the outer regions of my sockets. Narrow fissures so deep I'm sure I could slip dimes into them and they'd stay. My goatee and mustache have turned into a full three-day, salt-and-pepper beard, and my usually shaved head is sprouting new growth that not only doesn't hide the bullet-sized scar that resides beside my right earlobe, but somehow accentuates it.

Look at me...I tried to blow my brains out once.

It dawns on me that my head is pounding and my mouth tastes like an ashtray. I'm hungover. Crap, I hate hangovers. I'm thirty-plus-thousand feet up in the air, trapped inside a plane that's rocking all over the cosmos, and I'm hungover and apparently under arrest...excuse me...under *suspicion* of being a quote, "domestic terrorist," unquote, and I'm hungover.

The perfect start to the perfect day.

The water shuts off by itself. A nice, green feature of modern-day air travel. I pull some paper towels from the dispenser, wipe my face off.

How did I get here, and why don't I remember it?

Because I'm a head case with a small piece of .22 caliber bullet lodged in my brain. That's why I can't remember.

But that's not exactly right.

I do remember some things.

Some. Things.

Coming home from Lanie's bar, still drunk from the New York Giants' last-second win over the division rival Dallas Cowboys, assuring them their first playoff berth in three years. Drunk and feeling no pain due to a half dozen shots of Jack and maybe, ummm, a dozen beers. I'd lost count after six. One of those late-fall football Sunday afternoons spent on a barstool at Lanie's Grille that eventually turned into one of those juicy Sunday nights, since I'm unemployed, have no girlfriend, no child to take care of, and no reason other than basic bodily functions to get up in the morning. Especially on a Monday. One of those rarer-than-rare blocks of time where the future was my oyster—but quickly turned into a clam when, upon arriving back at my riverside loft, I noticed an envelope sticking out of a stack of unread mail on my kitchen island.

A letter from the IRS, addressed to me.

A notice for payment for back taxes in the amount of five Gs and change. A letter identical to three notices I've already received and paid out over the past twelve months. If I didn't know any better, I'd say the IRS was hounding me, baiting me, terrorizing me.

It's all coming back to me now, like a badly planned murder.

I see myself sitting slightly out of balance on the rickety barstool at the kitchen island inside my loft while my skin begins to peel itself away from my flesh and bones. I see steam pouring out my ears while I reposition my entire body weight on the stool and begin typing up an e-mail to the woman from the IRS whose job it is to handle my delinquent account. The same woman who, for the past year, has been haunting my dreams more stubbornly than my own impending death, than the thought of rotting in the lowest level of hell, than the still-vivid face of Lola, my ex-sig other, who ran off to strike up a new relationship with her old boyfriend.

Doris E. Walsh, IRS auditor.

I've never seen Doris in the flesh, but I couldn't help but picture a great white whale dressed in a too-tight polyester suit, hair pinned up, a black mustache shading her upper lip. Thick-framed cat-eyed glasses would cover beady little eyes and, of course, horns would protrude from the top of her skull while a small scar might be implanted on the scalp that reads "666." The entrance code to the Inferno. The PIN to eternal damnation.

But then, maybe I was being a little harsh. Doris was just doing her job, after all. A horrid job, collecting money for her federal boss.

My laptop was sitting out on the counter, booted up and ready. Positioning index fingers on the keypad, I began to type.

Dear Ms. Walsh,

I don't have any money. I didn't have any money the last time you hounded me for it, so I went to the bank and took out a loan for the five Gs you extorted from me then. I'm still paying on that loan and said financial institution surely won't lend me more money to give to you. I'm not only unemployed at the moment, but I can't collect unemployment insurance since I work for myself. I live off a small disability pension care of the New York State Law Enforcement Officers Union 82, along with a small Albany Police Department retirement account released early to me after I screwed up an attempt to blow my brains out.

Last year I made approximately forty thousand dollars as a private detective, most of which was paid to me in cash, which I assumed would not have to go reported to your organization. How was

I supposed to know I would be 1099'd later on by more than one conscientious client?

Read my lips, Doris: I don't have any fucking money!

Since I can't possibly pay you, and since you have a job to perform and a boss to answer to, tell you what I'm going to do. I'm going to head out to Lowe's and purchase several lengths of metal pipe along with some black powder and some simple detonators. Then I'm going to put one pipe bomb in your boss's mailbox, another under his car, and one more in his locker at whatever country club he belongs to. And he does belong to a country club, am I right, Doris? Yes indeed, I'm going to blow up your boss and at the same time send a message to all the terrorized and overtaxed good citizens of the United States.

The message?

"They say you can't escape death and taxes, but I've somehow managed to do both, on more than one occasion. And now I'd rather die again than shell out another dime."

Problem solved for both you and me, Doris. No more boss, no more overdue back taxes, no more threats of prison time, no more pressure on you to collect them from me.

Sincerely,

Richard "Dick" Moonlight, Concerned US Citizen

Standing before the mirror in the airplane lavatory, I recall the letter. Recall every word. All it takes to recall a letter like that is a little concentration and a patch of smooth air outside this airborne tuna can/death trap.

Exactly what happened next is not so easy to remember.

I was drunk. But I do remember sitting on that rickety barstool that I rescued from the ashes of the bar I owned for a few months: Moonlight's Moonlit Manor. The stool wasn't safe, its four legs wobbly, barely able to hold my weight. But you know how tough it can be to get rid of a piece of furniture? And barstools cost money.

I remember writing that letter, then sitting up straight, feeling the dizziness in my head and the sway of the stool. I read the letter maybe five times in a row and laughed out loud every time I read it.

I might have a bullet in my brain and I might have been drinking Jack and beer all afternoon and evening, but I wasn't stupid. I was perfectly aware that I couldn't actually *send* that letter to dear old Doris E. Walsh. Not without the FBI, the CIA, Homeland Security, the APD, the devil, and the good Lord himself coming down on me like a pack of wild dogs.

So, like a good, tax-paying American, broker-than-broke part-time private gumshoe, here's what I did: placing fingers back down onto the keyboard, I moved the cursor to Cancel. That's when I leaned forward on the barstool, placing more pressure on its legs. At the same time, dizziness filled my head. As you might have guessed, I'm not supposed to drink to excess with my damaged brain. That bullet frag might be tiny, but it's big enough to cause me to suffer short-term memory loss during times of stress. The bullet frag can also cause me to simply pass out, and at times, cause me to make wrong or illogical decisions.

Inhaling and exhaling, attempting to regain my equilibirum, I double-clicked on Cancel and another box appeared, this one offering me three choices:

SAVE AS DRAFT
Or...
KEEP WRITING
Or...
DISCARD

Naturally I shifted the cursor to Discard. But that's also when I began to feel myself falling backward, even before the crack of the stool's back legs registered with my damaged brain.

Instinct kicked in.

I reached out, desperate for something to hold on to, something to break my fall. Instead of grabbing the counter, I slapped my hands down onto the laptop keyboard before dropping like a rock. A split second later I found myself down on the wood floor, my drunk body resting on a pile of twisted metal and broken wood.

Heart pounding in my throat, I felt for broken bones. But as luck would have it, I'd landed on my glutes. I waited for the initial wave of pain to subside. Then I raised myself onto my knees, and from there, onto my feet. Besides the lumps and bruises on my ass and a throbbing pain in my skull, I was no worse off than usual.

I was contemplating one more beer and an Advil chaser just before heading to bed when I happened to glance at the computer screen. Something had appeared on the screen that sent more shockwaves throughout my body than that suddenly broken stool had when it collapsed beneath my body.

It was a shiny happy little green circle that contained an animated black checkmark. But the symbol was anything but shiny happy. Because placed beside it were two words spelled out in bold black letters. The letters spelled the words Message Sent.

More pounding on the door to compete with the bad wind buffeting this plane's fatigued sheet-metal skin.

"Come on, Moonlight!" Zumbo barks. "I need you back in your seat now."

The plane rocks up and down, violently. I'm shoved around the interior of that lav like a fish trapped inside a fishbowl. "Coming, Agent Zumbo!"

Turning toward the toilet, I bend down and pull up the seat.

The Airbus A300 trembles and jolts, knocking me against both walls inside the narrow lav.

"Move, Moonlight! Move it back to your seat and buckle in before we take a nosedive."

But I can't move.

I'm standing over the toilet, shrinking naked Johnson pinched between my index finger and thumb. I can't move, much less pee. I'm catatonic with fear.

The plane drops.

My head hits the ceiling.

Until the wings catch and now I'm on the floor, straddling the open stainless-steel toilet. There's a huge thump, and then screaming coming from outside the door. Something big and heavy has fallen.

It's got to be Zumbo.

Then comes an announcement over the PA:

"Ahhh, this is your captain speaking, ladies and gentlemen." Casual, lighthearted. Nice touch. "Not to be the bearer of bad news (*chuckle*), but we are encountering severe turbulence. We ask that you remain in your seats, seat belts buckled, and await further instructions from your flight attendants."

I don't want to die in a plane crash. I want to die in my bed in my sleep with Lola sleeping right beside me, her steady breaths caressing my final moment.

I pull myself up, turn, catch another glimpse in the mirror. A small gash above my right eye. A thin stream of blood oozing from it. No time for fixing it. I want out of here so that I can crash buckled in the safety of my seat.

I zip up my pants and open the door, step out into the cabin.

Zumbo is on the floor, pressed up against the corner of the galley, directly beside the emergency exit. Beside him, the cute little flight attendant is strapped into her booster seat.

"Take your seat *immediately*!" she orders. "We have an in-flight emergency!"

I cock my head and shoulder toward the NFL man turned federal cop. *What about him?*

"Never mind him. He fell and hit his head."

I stumble my way around the corner toward my seat. But that's when the Airbus rocks 'n' rolls again, bobbing up and down, shaking from side to side, like we're being bombarded by cannon fire on both flanks.

And then it happens.

Nosedive.

The nose of the plane dips toward planet earth.

I drop to the carpeted floor and grip the anchors of the two seats on either side of me. The g-forces yank me toward the tail of the plane. I feel like my heart is about to pop out of my chest. My torso and legs are no longer resting on the carpet as my body enters into a freefall along with the jet. I can make out the screams and shouts coming from the occupied seats a dozen rows ahead of me. The panicked and horrified voices compete with GE engines that scream and rev like they're about to blow.

How long does it take a nose-diving jetliner to make final contact with the solid ground from thirty thousand feet up in the air?

Three minutes. I read that somewhere. *Huffington Post.* Or was it Wikipedia?

I close my eyes, await the inevitable.

All three long minutes of it.

But we don't crash into the solid earth.

By some miracle of miracles, the plane rights itself, and I am once more on the carpet, both hands still gripping the seat anchors.

Behind me, a booted foot kicks the Vibram sole that protects my right foot.

"Get up! Get in your seat! Now!"

Zumbo.

I roll over. There's a black-and-blue lump that's freshly raised over his left eye. It reminds me of the cut above my right eye. There's something about his eyes. They're glazed over and sort of rolling around in their sockets while he tries to focus in on me. It's almost as if the real Zumbo is no longer really present and a sort of messed-up, head-banged, short-circuited version thereof has taken his place.

And to prove it, he pulls out his piece, aims it at me. At my face.

Coming up on him from behind, the flight attendant.

"Zumbo! No blood, no bullets, remember? It can't go down that way."

Yeah, no blood, no bullets, Zumbo. And what the fuck is she talking about? What way is it *supposed* to go down?

He turns to me, looks me in the eye. "Don't. Give. A. Fuck," he mumbles in this voice that sounds like an old vinyl record played at a too-slow speed. "You're. Dead. Sweetie."

I get back up on my feet, face the front of the plane.

"Zump!" I bark. "It's your head. You hit your fucking head. You're not yourself. I know what I'm talking about here. Put the gun away."

"Awwww, sweetie," he says, those wet eyes rolling around inside the sockets, a thin stream of drool running down his lower lip. "I love it when you beg."

Here's the deal: I'm scared.

Scared stiff and confused and hungover.

But my empty gut screams at me.

It screams *"Run!"*

But where the fuck to?

Zumbo wobbles out of balance. He thumbs back the pistol hammer and smiles.

Blood and bullets...

I run like hell.

CHAPTER 5

I lunge for the gray curtain, pull it up and over my hand, and pull it back down. For just a split second I see a scattering of passengers. All of them strapped to their seats. Some are crying, some praying with rosary beads in their hands, some folded over at the waist, their heads pressed between their legs like they're trying to kiss their asses good-bye.

Behind me I hear Zumbo's pounding footsteps.

I don't have time to focus on the scared-to-death passengers.

I run. Up the narrow aisle toward business class, through another gray curtain. But before I draw the curtain back, I steal a quick glance over my right shoulder only to see Zumbo coming for me, his automatic gripped in his right hand, barrel pointing toward the ceiling, glassy eyes focused on me like I'm a linebacker who's intercepted a pass meant for him. He's not running so much as he's hobbling as fast as he can.

Bad knees.

Bad head.

Bad day.

I draw the curtain and slip on through.

Like economy class, business class is sparsely populated with scared-shitless passengers. I see only the backs of their heads. I pay them no attention as I sprint toward the pilot's cabin.

It takes a couple of seconds to get there.

A flight attendant tries to stand in my way. This one is a man. He's got gray hair and a mustache to match, and he's wearing the traditional US Airways blue uniform of blue slacks, matching jacket, and tie.

"Please take your seat! We have an in-flight emergency!"

He peers into my eyes with all the power of his authority until he glances over my shoulder at the monster approaching me from behind.

"We most certainly do," I say.

From where I'm standing I can see beyond the luxury seats, and the rich people strapped into them, to the cockpit door. I brush past the attendant and make an all-out run for it. If I can get inside, I can grab the captain's attention and bolt the door closed behind me.

"Stop!" shouts the flight attendant.

"Get! Back!" screams Zumbo. "Sweetie! Dies!"

That's when a man jumps up from a port-side window seat positioned closest to the cockpit, pulls out what looks like a pistol, assumes combat position, and aims the barrel point-blank for my chest. He fires and a snakelike coil leaps from it at lightning speed, slaps my chest, and makes my entire body feel as if it's been dipped in hot lava.

The plane bounces and bucks.

The man who shot me falls to the floor directly in front of the cabin door. I try to maintain my balance, my posterior pressed up against an upright seatback. But the battle is lost before it begins. The beefy NFL monster behind me loses his balance and falls onto a first-class passenger who is screaming her lungs out and weeping.

I feel the plane falling again as my knees give out, and I lose consciousness.

CHAPTER 6

When I wake up I'm occupying the same bucket seat in the plane's aft where I woke up in the first place. The long gray curtain is back in place, Zumbo is seated beside me again, and once more I'm cuffed to his tree stump of a wrist. The cute red-headed flight attendant is nowhere to be seen, but the man who Tasered me is seated across the narrow aisle from Zumbo. I'm thinking he's the air marshal. Air marshal's got the Taser gun out. It's gripped in his right hand. I can also see that he's got Zumbo's automatic stuffed into his belt.

As for the turbulence, it seems to be history. Outside the window, nothing but blue skies. Peaceful, calm. But I know better than that. Zumbo is asleep. I can hear his snores. After our midair chase, I can't imagine how anyone, let alone an over-weight former New York Giant with bad knees and a bad head-ache, can sleep at a time like this. My guess is he's been forcibly medicated after pulling that little chase-the-rabbit stunt with me. Oh, the crazy, mindless things a head injury will cause a formerly logical thinker to do. Take it from me: Captain Head Case.

Air marshal shifts, leans forward to get a look at me.

I close my eyes, pretend to still be passed out.

A voice over the intercom. Captain's voice.

"Please be advised, ladies and gentlemen, that we will be making an emergency landing at JFK International Airport in approximately seven minutes. You'll have noticed that we have already begun our descent. Further instructions will be relayed to you by our flight attendants. We ask that you remain calm and cooperative for the remainder of the flight and follow strict emergency disembarking procedures, which include leaving all carry-on bags behind. When requested upon landing, utilize your closest emergency exit in a calm and orderly fashion. Thank you in advance for your cooperation, and thanks for choosing US Airways."

Seven minutes.

Out the corner of my eye I catch the flight attendant approaching the air marshal. I bet she thinks he's cute. I try to get a decent enough look at them by leaning forward so that I can see around Zumbo's giant, bulbous head. Here's what I see: the flight attendant reaches down for Zumbo's piece, which is still stuffed into the air marshal's crotch. I see her grip the piece and pull it toward her. She pulls back the bolt, checks to make sure a round is chambered, or perhaps no longer chambered, which is more likely the case. She closes the bolt, thumbs the clip release, and allows the clip to drop into her hand. Shoving the clip into her shirt pocket, she doesn't hand the piece back to the air marshal. Instead, she gently opens Zumbo's shirt and slides it back into his holster.

"Told you we shouldn't have let Zumbo pack his standard issue," she whispers. "He might have fucked this whole thing up."

The air marshal shrugs. "Far as Zumbo the Dumbo knows, Moonlight's a terrorist, an IRS bomber," he murmurs. "Then he gets his head hit and he turns into psycho boy. He played pro ball, remember? His brains are already scrambled, probably worse than Moonlight's. He comes to, Moonlight's on the loose. He goes all Action Jackson on a bad acid trip."

"Trying to get one hundred crew and passengers killed. Nice."

Cocking his head, working up a smirk. "All these people will have something to tell their grandchildren," the air marshal says. Mr. Bright Side.

"That turbulence was enough to tell their grandchildren."

"Yes, but it worked in your favor. I was able to put Moonlight down."

Zumbo grunts, bobs his head forward. My cue to lay my head back, resume passed-out position. But just as quickly as he stirs, the ex-fullback begins to snore again.

Through my lashes, I watch both the flight attendant and air marshal focus their gaze on us sleeping beauties. Or should I say *uglies*.

"I know Zumbo can sleep through anything even without being dosed. But how long will Moonlight be passed out like that?"

"Don't know," the air marshal says. "You got the body bag ready?"

She nods. "You might have killed him for real with that Taser. I know it's your job as AM, Kevin, but I'm supposed to take extreme care of his head. He can die from a stroke at any time even without the help of a Taser. And the FBI most certainly needs him alive."

"No further arguments from me, Agent," the air marshal comments.

"Soon as we land," she says, "you guys will be the first ones down those chutes. The car will be waiting for you, along with two NYPD blue-and-whites. I'll be right behind you."

"Gotcha, Chief."

The air marshal leans in toward the flight attendant/FBI agent, wraps his arms around her waist, and pulls her into him.

She pushes him off with a giggle. "Not here. Not on the job. Not at all. We're history, Kevin. We had a good run, but—"

"Don't embarrass the bureau, is that it?" Air Marshal Kevin grouses. "You're turbulence enough for one man. You're why I left the bureau."

She slaps his hand as she steps back into the galley, and the descending passenger jet enters into the thick cloud cover.

CHAPTER 7

Soon as we're through the thick gray cloud cover and the plane has once again stopped bucking like a bronco on speed, the Manhattan skyline comes into view, its towers looming over the horizon like giant steel-and-glass needles pinpricking the sky. The pilot makes a couple figure-eight revolutions in preparation for the emergency landing. I still feign sleep while the little flight attendant straps herself into the wall-mounted foldout seat just outside the galley.

My wrist jerks as Zumbo is jarred awake.

"Are we there yet?" he barks, swiping the drool from his mouth with the back of his good hand. The lump above his eye is more black and blue than before.

"Landing," answers the air marshal.

"Better than crashing," I say, pretending to have only now woken up.

Zumbo jerks his wrist, sending electric pain shooting up my right arm. "Shut up, sweetie," he spits. "Don't say another word."

I'm not sure if it's head-injured Zumbo speaking or the real-deal Zumbo. His words aren't slurred anymore, so I'm guessing the latter.

The pilot comes back on the PA then, tells us all to assume crash position while he lands the big bird on an out-of-the-way runway where emergency crews will be awaiting us.

Air Marshal Kevin leans forward, head between his legs.

"Don't be so fucking dramatic," Zumbo mocks. Then, "What about you, Moonlight, sweetie? You gonna tongue your nut sack good-bye too?"

I stare out the window onto water, which quickly turns into the brown terra firma of Queens. "I'll take whatever comes sitting up," I say, my heart jumping up into my throat.

Moonlight the terrified.

Terra firma fast becomes a runway. We feel the thump of the landing. Brakes quickly applied, we all lurch forward as the pilot parks the US Airways Airbus onto a wide expanse of tarmac.

We're not stopped for more than three seconds when we're greeted by a team of EMS vans, fire trucks, and cop cars. Flashers flashing. Sirens screaming.

"Unbuckle, Moonlight," Zumbo insists.

I do it.

"We're going for a ride." He pulls me up and out of my seat by the cuffs. I feel like my hand is about to be severed at the wrist. Maybe that's what he's going for.

Cute flight attendant/FBI agent unstraps herself, shoots up from her seat. Heading back into the galley, she comes back out with a rolled-up bag. I'm the son of a mortician. I know a body bag when I see one.

"You're not serious?" I say.

"Do it, Moonlight," Zumbo orders while the flight attendant, or whatever she is, rolls it out onto the floor. "Get in."

I just stare down at it.

"Now!"

Situation beyond my control. I'm powerless. Might as well be dead. I lay myself down, slip my left foot inside, followed by my torso, and then the rest of my body. The zipper is quickly zipped and my world turns black.

"Make even a peep, Moonlight," Zumbo warns, "and you'll never leave the body bag alive."

There's some real irony for you.

I don't speak as I hear what has to be the emergency exit opening and the loud pop of the emergency chute inflating. What happens next happens fast. I'm lifted off the floor and tossed onto the chute for a fast ride, straight down. My heels hit the tarmac hard, my knees buckling, my breath escaping my lungs.

From up above I can hear Zumbo laughing. I hear him scream, "Geronimo!"

I hear the commotion that a whale of a man makes when he slides down an emergency chute.

"Whaddaya think, Moonlight?" he shouts upon crash-landing. "Wanna go again?"

Too bad he didn't land on his head. Maybe this time the already head-banged big beast would have lost consciousness for a while. Maybe for the rest of his life.

I try not to speak. Not because it would constitute a peep. But my breath is still knocked out of me.

Then the sound of a car or van pulling up. I'm lifted off the tarmac and shoved into the back of the vehicle, the door closing behind me. From there, we speed off, rooftop sirens blaring.

Once again, I'm dead.

Lord help me, I'm dead.

PART II

CHAPTER 8

I've been here before.

In a dozen other buildings in a dozen different towns. But always the same setting. As if to add some color and comfort to an FBI interview room would somehow go against company policy or what Hollywood would want us to believe in one of its B-level crime thriller movies.

Instead, what we've got is four walls, no windows other than a four-by-eight one-way mirror located in the wall opposite my right shoulder. I'm seated in the usual metal chair at the usual metal table, my wrists cuffed and chained to the usual round metal disk that protrudes from the underside of said metal table. That way they can be sure I won't kill them all should I suddenly enter into a rage. OK, maybe I tried to shoot myself once, but I'm not about to pull a stunt like Zumbo did on the plane just because my head's a little off.

Seated beside me is Agent Zumbo. He's sipping on a coffee and enjoying a jelly doughnut that he's lifted from off a plate of a dozen others just like it.

Dunkin' Donuts.

There's a long piece of white surgical tape stuck to his forehead. The surgical tape is holding a piece of thick gauze in place over the egg-shaped lump and apparent concussion he suffered during our severely turbulent flight.

The cut above my forehead hasn't been touched. But it has stopped bleeding. I'm guessing they figure it's only a scratch.

Seated across from us is the agent who apparently posed as Cute Little Flight Attendant, whose name I have discovered is Vanessa Crockett. She's got a nice figure and no doubt she intends to keep it, which is probably why she is abstaining from the doughnuts, although I'm getting a kick out of watching her eyes shift from the pile of white jelly-filled doughy goodness every two or three seconds.

Conspicuously missing from the party, the mustached Air Marshal Kevin, who I can only assume is back to flying and protecting the friendly skies.

"In five seconds, everyone," comes a tinny hidden speaker voice from behind me. *"Can you please say something, Mr. Moonlight, so we can check the levels?"*

"There once was a fellow McSweeny," I recite, "who spilled some gin on his weenie..."

"That works for me."

Zumbo must get a kick out of that 'cause he bursts out laughing, his round mouth covered in white powder. "For a little man, you crack me up, sweetie. You really do."

"Can we just get this started?" Agent Crockett barks. "I'm exhausted from that dreadful flight, and I wanna take a bath."

Well, fuck me. She had to put that image in my head, right? Her naked body, resting in a pool of hot, steamy water and bubble bath. Heart be still.

"Good to go, Agents."

Zumbo grabs another doughnut, takes a sip of coffee.

Crockett pushes her chair out, stands up.

Zump...Zumbo's nickname bestowed upon him by his fellow New York Giants. Whenever he'd run over a middle linebacker the television broadcaster would shout, "You've just been Zumped!" The fans picked up on it too and so did the stadium JumboTron. Picture a giant cartoon caricature of Zump running over a skinny little cartoon defensive player, the word ZUMPED! cascading across the screen in big bold letters, the entire stadium shouting "ZUMPED!" in unison.

The old fullback wipes his powder- and jelly-stained right hand on his pant leg.

"Aren't you gonna offer me a doughnut?" I pose.

Zumbo slaps my arm. The solid rock of a hand sends a shockwave throughout my torso. "Yo," he says, "play right."

"Kidnapping and physical torture," I hiss. "All this is gonna make a great lawsuit, let me tell you."

Agent Crockett turns away from the table, raises her right hand over her shoulder, waves it dismissively, like she's about to say, *See ya!*

"Oh, Moonlight, spare it. We don't give a rat's ass about lawsuits. We don't have to. When it comes to domestic and international terrorism and the threat thereof, we enjoy an almost unlimited autonomy, so long as it's in the best interest, health, and security of the GP."

"That comes as a relief, actually, Agent Crockett. Save me a fortune in lawyer fees. You fabricate that severe turbulence too? In the best interest of the GP?"

"Shut *up*, little man." Zumbo slaps me again. It hurts again too.

"Zump," Crockett scolds, "please don't hit the suspect. And no, Mr. Moonlight, that turbulence was the real deal."

"Shackled suspect," I add. "So aside from that stupid letter I wrote, why am I here?"

The female agent peers into the one-way mirror, then turns to face me once more. "Mr. Moonlight, do you recall a former APD detective by the name of Dennis Clyne?"

The name hits me upside the head. Less than a year ago he helped relieve me of a gang of Russian thugs who, along with the father of Lola, my then-girlfriend, were going to kill me if I didn't produce a certain flash drive containing sensitive nuclear weapons secrets on it. Rogue nuclear warhead locations, to be more precise, that landed on the black market following the end of the Cold War. The short of it is that I never realized I was in possession of said flash drive until I discovered that it had been safely stored under a table in Moonlight's Moonlit Manor.

In the end, Lola's father was killed and the bar burned to the ground. Lola ran off with her ex-boyfriend. Dude who goes by the name of Christian Barter and who also happens to be a special agent for the FBI and the biological father of the now-deceased son she was forced to give up at birth, since she was only sixteen at the time. And Detective Clyne, whom I personally and, yes, illegally entrusted the flash drive to, bolted the country with it.

A shitload to sort out, I know. Try *living* it.

"I remember Clyne," I admit. "How can I not?"

"Do you have any idea of his whereabouts?" Agent Crockett pushes.

"Word up is that he's somewhere in Europe."

"Where exactly, sweetie?" asks Zumbo.

I try to sit back. But my shackled hands won't allow it. And my right wrist stings when I pull on it against the steel cuff. I turn to eye his round, doughnut-stuffed head. "Oh jeepers,

Agent Zumbo," I say, "Clyne asked me not to reveal that when he placed his last personal call to me a few days ago." Rolling my eyes. "Come on, Zump man, how the fuck should I know?"

He slaps me again. On the fleshy part of the upper arm, above the bicep. Does it with that heavyweight Super Bowl ring out front. I fall most of the way off the chair.

"That's 'Agent Zumbo' to you, little man," he says.

"So it's true, then, that you and Clyne are in communication?" asks Agent Crockett.

Christ almighty, what happened to her little mandate about not hitting and/or abusing the suspect? The hot little Crockett appears to have forgotten all about it. I exhale, shake my head. "I was being facetious."

"Which is it, Moonlight?" the female agent shouts. "Yes or no?"

My head is beginning to spin. Not a good sign. It means my blood pressure is up. When my pressure is up, a lot of blood flows through my brain and it makes the sliver of bullet lodged inside the gray matter press up against the cerebral cortex. It means I'm in danger of passing out, at best, and at worst, falling into a coma. For now I'll just take deep breaths and tackle their silly questions as accurately as I can.

"That would be a big fat *no*," I assure her. "So, let me clarify something here. I really don't get to see a lawyer?"

"What do you need a lawyer for, Moonlight?" Crockett poses, like I'm asking to speak to the president. "You're not accused of anything. Nor have you been arrested. We're just talking is all."

"And I'm just shackled for no reason, having been kidnapped, Tasered, and taken to New York City entirely against my will."

"The plane almost crashed and you went haywire," Zumbo interjects, like he didn't lose it at all himself after suffering a head-on collision with the hard US Airways interior during a moment of severe turbulence.

"Thus the reason for your cuffs, Mr. Moonlight," Crockett explains. "Also, when we originally, and might I add, politely, asked you to accompany us to New York, you went ballistic. You had to be restrained."

I'm trying to recall their coming to my door early this morning. But I have no recollection whatsoever. Considering the amount of alcohol I imbibed yesterday, I must have still been drunk.

"You don't remember, do you, Moonlight?"

I shake my head.

"My brain—"

"We know, we know." The pretty agent nods. "It's not always right."

Crockett turns back to the mirror. "Pictures!" she barks.

A second later the door opens, and a short, thin man enters. He's holding a manila folder, which he sets down on the table. When he leaves, closing the door behind him, the female agent opens the folder to reveal a series of eight-by-ten full-color glossies.

"Recognize any of these, Moonlight?" she asks, slapping down the stack before me.

The top pic is of a man. A tall man with broad shoulders, dressed all in black. His head's been shaved, leaving only a small cropping of hair. He has an equally cropped beard to match. He's lost considerable weight, but I have no doubt about the identity of the man in the picture. "Clyne," I say.

"So you do recognize him?"

"I just told you that!"

Zumbo, slapping the back of my head. "Be nice."

When the shockwave abates, I say, "Yes, ma'am, I recognize him."

"Nice touch, sweetie," Zumbo adds. "Need more of that 'ma'am' stuff 'round here. Fact, we need more mams 'round here, period." He finishes with a wink at Crockett, who pretends to ignore the gesture.

"You should be aware, Mr. Moonlight," she goes on, "that you were the last man in the US to have any direct contact with Clyne prior to his sudden disappearance. We also know that you personally handed him the flash drive in question when it was your solemn duty and obligation as a former officer of the law to produce it for federal authorities. Namely, Agent Christian Barter. We further know that you withheld information about the illegal handoff that would have aided both local and federal law enforcement, leading us to believe, Mr. Moonlight—"

"That you are totally fucked." Zumbo, laughing so hard he's about to fall out of his chair.

But he's right. I'm fucked. And they know it. We sit in a silence so pregnant you can practically feel the baby kicking.

Until I raise up my head and say, "Ummm, would it help if I said I was sorry?"

I close my eyes, cringe, and brace myself because I know what's coming. Another slap. Against my left shoulder. Harder this time, the Super Bowl ring indenting itself into my flesh. When I open my eyes I'm down on the floor on my side, my cuffed hands hanging above my head from where the cuff chain is attached to the underside of the metal table.

"You been Zumped, sweetie!"

Fucking Zumbo.

He helps me back up and pats me on the back like I'm a teammate he's just crushed all in the name of good sportsmanship. I run my fingers over abraded wrists and pray that, at this point, my hands don't simply fall off.

"OK," I say, "so what is it you want from me, Crockett, besides a death certificate?"

She pulls the top photo off the stack, sets it onto the table. Using her manicured index finger like a pointer, she points to the man seated in the middle. "Recognize the person in this shot, Moonlight?"

This man is also dressed in black. He's taller than Clyne, clean-shaven, with trimmed dirty blond hair that's streaked with gray. In the picture he's seated in between Clyne and someone else I recognize. The someone else I recognize is wearing a black leather jacket. Her long black hair is lush and parted over her right eye. She's wearing white plastic Jackie O sunglasses, tight white jeans, and long, knee-high boots. She's my ex-girlfriend, Lola. The man to her left is Barter, her new boyfriend and the man who fathered the child she gave up for adoption at birth in the mid-1980s when they were both only sixteen years old. A child named Peter Czech, who became a nuclear engineer and a spy for the Russian government. A man paralyzed from the waist down who originally owned the flash drive in question prior to his untimely death.

Crockett begins going through the stack of photos. They are all the same. Shots of Lola, Barter, and Clyne sitting at a table at a café somewhere. Looks like Europe.

"Those other people look familiar to you too, Moonlight?"

"It's Lola Ross," I say and exhale, "and a colleague of yours. Agent Christian Barter. I'm assuming you know Barter through agency circles, Agent Crockett?"

"*Former FBI agent*," she stresses. "And yes, I've met former Agent Barter, on numerous occasions during my occasional trips up to the Albany field office, Moonlight."

I'd sit back in my chair and sigh if the chain length would allow it. But it won't.

"What do you want from me?" I repeat.

What do you want so badly you're willing to kidnap me, hit me, chain me up, Taser me, and nearly shoot me while in midflight thirty thousand feet above the solid fucking ground in order to get it?

Crockett turns to the mirror like it's alive and breathing.

"What do you think?" she says aloud.

"*Tell him now*," says a tinny PA voice.

Mirror, mirror, on the wall, who's the most fucked-over one of us all?

Richard "Dick" Moonlight. That's who.

CHAPTER 9

"There's no easy way to tell you this, Moonlight," Crockett says, "so I'm just gonna say it: we require your services in a matter of extreme national security."

"Maybe you should call James Bond."

I brace myself, fully expecting to be Zumped. But it doesn't come.

"We want you to locate Clyne and Barter for us, Mr. Moonlight. And more importantly, we want you to locate the flash drive, and then forward us the information we need in order to seize and detain them both, in cooperation with our friends at Interpol."

"See?" Zumbo says. "Easy-peasy." He's munching on his third doughnut since we started.

"Easy-peasy," I repeat. "And where am I supposed to locate them?"

She comes close to the table, leans down into it. She places an extended index finger on the photo closest to me. "Recognize any of these buildings in the foreground and background, Moonlight?"

I take a good look at the picture.

Cobbled street. Cobbled square, to be more precise. A big white-and-black marble building in the background. To the right, a café. People walking, dressed in stylish jackets and sweaters, carrying plastic designer shopping bags of one kind or another. Fashionable women in short skirts and colorful tights. Men dressed in black mostly, wearing sunglasses, scarves wrapped around their necks.

"Florence, Italy," I say, looking up.

"Been there?"

"Couple of times. Once as a boy, not long after my mother died. Later, right out of college."

"Our records indicate as much. Which is also why we're talking now."

My eyes go wide. *Enlighten me, please.*

"We have a bit of a proposal for you, Moonlight."

A proposal. I'm cuffed and shackled to a metal table that must weigh half a ton and she's talking about a proposal.

"Do tell, Ms. Agent." Closing my eyes, waiting for the slap...that never comes. Zump must be getting bored with me. Or he's undergoing a sugar crash to go with that concussion.

"Clyne's a simple APD dick. His connections reach about as far as the Hudson River on one side and the state capitol on the other. Or translated another way, he can't begin to sell the flash drive on his own. Not to the right peeps, anyway. He's small potatoes. Therefore, we believe that Clyne approached Barter in order to open up his world to potential buyers. As an FBI agent, Barter would have unlimited connections not just in the States but all over the world. We believe that Barter agreed to whatever deal Clyne offered him, and that he is now attempting to facilitate the sale of the flash drive to one or more of these, let's call them, more worldly connections. Agenting the sale, if you will. A sale that could run in the hundreds of millions of euros or dollars. All cash transactions aside, once that flash drive is sold and out of their hands, there's no telling where it will land. But if it lands in the hands of a terrorist organization, the free world could be at serious risk."

"But I'm just a hack private eye with a bullet in his brain and a habit of forgetting things."

"We know from our research that your ex-girlfriend, Dr. Ross, and Barter are no longer the content peas in a pod they seemed to be while sharing in their mutual grief for their dead son, Peter Czech. We believe they are very much at odds with one another, especially in light of Barter's newfound hobby of facilitating the sale of rogue nuclear weapons and decades of nuclear secrets to the highest bidder."

I feel my blood beginning to simmer, my head beginning to buzz from adrenaline. Lola's in trouble. Could be that she's been in trouble for a while now, and I was just too blind to see it. I have no idea when she started seeing Barter again, how many weeks and months she spent in my bed while also seeing the FBI agent on the side. No idea when they started sleeping together on a regular basis. All I know is that for the few minutes we were all in one another's presence immediately following the death of their son, Peter, Lola and Barter seemed to be in love. They shared the biological bond of a son they never got the chance to see grow up, much less get to know as a young adult. They shared only in the grief of watching him die. And now, in the wake of that death and the horrible emotional riptide that's swept through their bodies, souls, and brains, they've both fled the country. Barter has willingly stripped himself of everything he ever committed himself to as a lawman. Or so it seems. Such is the power of a traumatic event like losing a son you never knew. Or fuck, what the hell do I know, maybe he's been a rotten son of a bitch all along.

"Lola's being held against her will, isn't she?"

"It's certainly possible."

"Which is it?" I demand. "Yes or no?"

Agent Crockett breathes in, then out. "No, in that we've spotted her making her way about the city on her own, shopping, eating, walking, drinking coffee at the open-air cafés."

"But…"

"But yes, in that we feel that if she were to attempt to leave Florence on her own, Barter and Clyne would go after her."

"So where do I come in?"

"Lola loves you, or *loved* you anyway. She will trust you with the location of the flash drive."

"You want me to *use* Lola."

"Yes, but we also want you to protect her from Barter and everything he has become capable of since the death of his son. In the end, you will have done both her and your country a great service."

"And if I refuse?"

"We prosecute you for terrorizing flight 7106 from Albany to New York, for one. Second, we prosecute you for having assisted not only in the withholding of evidence crucial to national security, but also in handing it over to a man intent on betraying the United States of America."

"Clyne was a real cop at the time," I plead.

"Tell it to that lawyer you keep threatening us with, sweetie," Zumbo interjects.

"Third," Crockett says, "we have your IRS pipe bomb letter. That terroristic act alone can send you away for a good, long time."

I pull on my cuffs. I feel the sting in my wrist. On one hand I would love nothing more than to try to win Lola's heart back.

On the other, I could get myself and her killed while trying to do it. I might be a head case, but I'm smart enough to realize just how dangerous that little flash drive could be in the wrong hands. Without giving them the benefit of hearing it, I'm on the FBI's side, regardless of their methods of convincing me to join their cause.

"When, ah, would I be leaving for this little trip back to Florence?"

"Tomorrow morning."

I nod. *That soon...* "Think you might unlock me now, seeing as I'm sort of working with you?"

She tosses Zumbo a nod.

He reaches over, unlocks both the shackles and the cuffs, which he sets onto the table. "Sorry about that, Moonlight," he offers. "Standard operating procedure."

"I'll add it to my legal list of grievances." I stand. "Do I get to make a request?"

"Doesn't mean we have to honor it," Crockett assures. "But ask away anyway."

I clear my throat. "In the event that I'm able to retrieve the flash drive for you, can you perhaps see to it that my IRS tax bill with Mrs. Doris E. Walsh is taken care of in full?"

Crockett shifts her big brown eyes to the one-way glass as if she can see right through it. Nodding but frowning, she says, "Done. That is, if you produce the flash drive for us."

"What about my clothes, and luggage, a computer, a phone?"

She holds up her hand. *We got it covered.*

"Agent Zumbo here is happy to take you shopping for all the above, plus new clothes." She smiles. For the first time since we entered the interview room. She also does something that catches me slightly off guard. She gently takes hold of my right hand and runs her fingers over the abrasions on my wrist, like she's trying to heal them. "It's Florence. You'll of course want to look dashing, to say the least. Someone that any woman, perhaps even Lola, will fall head over heels for."

"Dashing," I repeat, feeling the heat coming off her fingers and onto my scrapes and scratches. In my head I'm seeing her rebuking Air Marshal Kevin when he tried to cop a feel on the plane. I'm hearing her words about their affair being over and his having left the FBI because of it. He referred to her as turbulent. A storm-driven woman. I might be irreparably in love with Lola, but standing there in the interview room, I can't help but think that Crockett is my type of woman. A black widow kind of woman, capable not only of breaking hearts, but rendering them into so much mush.

Moonlight the hopeless.

"Agent Zumbo will accompany you from here," she adds, "while you still have the bulk of the afternoon."

She releases my wrist. I almost offer up my other wrist, but I figure it's better to cut and run while I have the opportunity.

Zumbo slides back his chair, gets up, and together we head toward the door. But before we get there, I turn back around.

"Oh, by the way, Agent Crockett," I say. "I really, really hate to fly. I thought you would have figured that one out by now."

Another smile. She's good at this smiling stuff, it turns out.

"We have," she says, reaching into her bag and pulling out a small orange pharmaceutical bottle. "Valium." She tosses me the bottle.

I grab it out of midair, stuff it into my jacket pocket. "Wow, drugs, money, and a free trip to sunny Italy."

"Must be your lucky day, sweetie," Zumbo says, before slapping me on the ass.

CHAPTER 10

The FBI's mission to get their precious flash drive back begins right away. Turns out Zumbo isn't just one hell of a former Giant fullback; he's also a giant shopper. He drags me all over the city. Drags me to Bergdorf's, Macy's, Abercrombie and Fitch, the Gap, for pants, shirts, running shoes, running clothes, sunglasses, two new bathing suits, luggage, and even a new black leather jacket that cost the FBI more than a thousand bucks.

He also brings me to a stylist named, get this: Bruno. Bruno trims my facial hair to just a small, neat shadow, and the hair on my head to barely a growth above the scarred skin. I look so good, the black-bearded Bruno can't take his eyes off of me.

Along the way we stop at just about every street corner hot-dog vendor for "a snack and a rest." Man, can Zumbo eat. But all that walking on concrete is not kind to his bad knees. The lump on his forehead is not as swollen as it was this morning. And all symptoms of the temporary psychosis that led him to pulling his service piece on me in midflight seem to have abated. But that doesn't mean I'm about to turn my back on him anytime soon.

Later in the day he books me a suite at the Gramercy Park Hotel, upping my bill with the feds by an entire grand. Add to that a bottle of fine red wine, a six-pack of Peroni beer (to get into the Italian spirit), a fresh pack of Marlboro Lights, some cooked brie, and a platter of cold jumbo shrimp, and I'm really beginning to like my new job as a deputized FBI agent, even if I haven't been officially sworn in as anything other than a citizen who either retrieves a very dangerous flash drive or faces prison time himself.

Zumbo leaves me to my lonesome after reminding me that I'm being watched at all times. But I figure I'm still allowed to take in a run along the East River. Fact is, maintaining my daily exercise routine is a priority and is strictly enforced by my general practitioner, who is always concerned about my circulation. That bullet fragment lodged inside my brain not only runs the risk of shifting one day, causing instant paralysis or death, but a blood clot can also form around it should my circulation not be operating at peak performance. And peak performance means constant exercise.

I run south toward downtown until I come to the giant stone stanchions that support the Williamsburg Bridge, where I about-face and head back to the hotel. I pop the top on a Peroni beer, take it with me into the shower, and despite the surreal nature of my newfound lifestyle, try to think realistically about the job that lies ahead. Mostly I try to recall Clyne and what I really know about him.

Detective Clyne first visited me in the hospital barely a day after I died a clinical death and underwent an out-of-body experience that told me my significant other, Lola, was seeing another man. From where my soul floated above the hospital bed, I saw Lola and this new man. Saw them practically making out over my dead body. Turns out that new man was really her old high school love, Christian Barter.

But as for Clyne, I recall a sort of dumpy-in-the-gut, sad-looking man who bore the scars of a recent separation from his wife after she'd taken off with her personal trainer. I pegged him right away as a heavy drinker who knew what it meant to medicate himself night in and night out in order to sleep, but more importantly, to forget and to eliminate his dreams. He had sad, deep brown eyes, a high forehead, and on occasion he would reveal a smile that told me he'd known happiness and, now that he didn't have it anymore, he missed it terribly.

He took a liking to me and helped me out by offering me protection from a gang of Russian mobsters disguised in President Obama masks who were bent on torturing me in the hopes of finding the flash drive, or what they mistranslated as a "fleshy box."

What I didn't realize at the time was that Clyne had other plans.

He wanted the flash drive for himself.

He was determined to get it, and to use it to start a new life somewhere else in a new country. It was his intention to flip the bird on the world—the world he'd built with his cheating wife and the cops—by going rogue. Problem is, the flash drive he took off with was said to contain not only information concerning the location of millions in unmarked euros and dollars stored in numerous Swiss accounts; it also revealed both the locations of misplaced Soviet-era nuclear warheads and sensitive US nuclear secrets that would be worth hundreds of millions to interested buyers. Not the Russians, necessarily, but the Iranians perhaps, maybe the North Koreans, and even the Pakistanis. Or maybe some unknown terrorist group who would like to get their hands on the information and use it to blow something up, like, say, New York City or Los Angeles.

So long as Clyne has that flash drive he's considered one of the most wanted men in the world. Now so is my girlfriend's new "old" squeeze, Agent Barter. Or so my new FBI friends tell me. I wonder if that technically makes Lola wanted also. Whatever the case, I've been trusted with infiltrating this new threesome, and with ultimately finding the flash drive.

An untrustworthy head case like me.

Makes total sense, doesn't it?

CHAPTER 11

When my beer is done, so is my shower. I'm drying off and anticipating some of the food the FBI has laid out for me and what, these days, has become a rare cigarette...when I hear the hotel room door open.

I also hear it shut, the deadbolt engage.

Gut instinct tells me to grab my automatic. But I'm totally naked and equally unarmed. I take a quick survey of the bathroom to see if there's something I can use as a weapon. The closet thing I can find is a drinking glass.

I wrap the bath towel around my waist, and then pick up the drinking glass. I hold it in the palm of my hand like a rock, the thick, heavy bottom pointing out. Swallowing a breath, I open the bathroom door, step out.

She's standing in the center of the floor, a dark brown leather bag slung over her shoulder. She's not wearing her FBI Windbreaker right now. She's wearing, instead, a black silk blouse that's unbuttoned enough to reveal some cleavage and just a hint of a black lace bra. Victoria's Secret maybe. Her mini-skirt is also black and tight-fitting. The heels on her long black leather boots make her almost as tall as me. Shoulder-length hair parted neatly above her right temple, deep brown eyes, and moist red lips make me want to take her into my arms, toss her onto the bed.

But I'm dressed in only a bath towel, and it's all I can do not to keep from proving to her how glad I am to see her. But a quick peek down at the pup tent emerging from my midsection tells me I'm having little success controlling Mother Nature.

"I let myself in," she says.

"We can see that," I say.

She can't help but work up a grin. "I hope these accommodations are to your liking."

"Well beyond expectations. You're trying to get on my good side."

"We at the FBI wanted to prove we aren't entirely uncivil when it comes to kidnapping in the name of national security."

"Feel free to kidnap me anytime."

She smiles and sets the bag onto the desk chair, takes notice of the food and the wine laid out there. Two long-stem drinking glasses came with the wine. Why hadn't I noticed that before? The wine has been uncorked for breathing. I never noticed that, either.

"Well, Moonlight," Agent Crockett says and sighs, "you gonna stand there in your bath towel or are you going to pour a girl a glass of wine?"

I make it two steps toward the bottle before I grab her hand and pull her into me. My towel comes off, drops to my feet. I'm standing at the end of the bed. Exposed. Both heads.

"My, my, Moonlight," she says, staring me up and down. The look on her face is dead serious. Like she's about to arrest me instead of seduce me. So much for professionalism.

I crawl onto the bed, pull her down beside me, begin unbuttoning her shirt. She closes her eyes, issues a slight moan, her chest heaving in and out.

"This is what I kept seeing in my head during our interview," she whispers in my ear.

I cup her bra-covered breast with my right hand, pinch her erect nipple through the fabric.

"Sure this is a very good idea?" I whisper. "We've become coworkers."

But it's too late for that now as I have her shirt entirely unbuttoned, and I'm kissing the parts of her pert breasts that aren't covered by her bra.

"I don't care what the FBI thinks," she moans. "You're on *my* time now."

I think about reminding her that just a few hours ago she ordered me cuffed and shackled to a metal table inside an FBI interrogation room, and that if I don't produce Clyne's flash drive for her, she will have me arrested. But then, who wants to talk shop at a time like this?

I kiss her on the mouth.

"Lights on or off?" she poses, coming up for air.

"Does it matter?" I answer.

We leave the lights on.

CHAPTER 12

Later on we're eating shrimp and drinking wine in bed. Or Agent Crockett is drinking wine and I'm having another beer. I attempt to light a cigarette but immediately reconsider when she shoots me this tight-as-a-tick expression with her official agent face.

"Don't even think about it, Moonlight."

What happened to Dick?

Clearly our little tryst was just that. Little. But it's quality not quantity that counts in these matters. And Vanessa Crockett showed some skills, let me tell you.

Pulling her shirt back on, along with her panties, Agent Crockett reappears for me by getting back down to all business. Set by the bed is the leather shoulder bag she brought into the room with her earlier. She hoists up the bag, opens it, and pulls out one of those sleek, slick, super-thin new Mac laptops that I can't even begin to afford. Next she pulls out a passport, a wallet filled with credit cards and cash. Both euros and dollars. Clearly the FBI seems to have covered their bases.

I open the passport, glance at the photo. It's me from my days as a cop. How the FBI acquired it I have no idea. But then, I'm not surprised they acquired it either.

"We have a source who tells us that your ex-significant other shows up now and again at a bar located not far from the Santa Maria Novella piazza." Now clicking on a map of Florence and enhancing so we get a real-time satellite view of the very square she's talking about. "Right there," she adds, using her index finger as a pointer. "Establishment called Harry's Bar. Right on the river."

"I know it. Hemingway used to drink at the one up in Venice."

"Florence is small and very walkable, if you recall."

I do recall. You can walk from one end to the other in fifteen minutes.

"You want me to have a few drinks at Harry's, I take it. Find a way to reintroduce myself to Lola."

She nods.

"That would be the strategy. Let's hope she's willing to trust you enough with the location of the flash drive."

"What if she figures out immediately that I'm working for the cops, and splits?"

"Then job over. We'll fly you right back. But..."

It's one of those dangling *Buts*...

"But we don't believe that will happen. We believe that, given the chance to make her escape, she'll want to accompany you out of the country. We have a ticket waiting for her. Just make sure she has her passport. Interpol has been alerted, and she will be allowed through airport security without a hitch."

"Gotcha. But what if the flash drive isn't so readily available?"

"Listen, if it's hidden inside a safety deposit box in a local bank, we want to know. If it's hidden inside a vault, we want to know the combination or, at the very least, a verifiable location. But if it's located inside a sock in Clyne's underwear drawer, we want you to find a way to get in and steal it. The point, Moonlight, is to convince Lola to reveal what she knows."

"I'll seduce her with my charm and good looks." Moonlight the confident.

"Watch yourself," she warns. "One danger will be your falling back in love with your ex. You must maintain enough focus and control to get the job done. Keep that brain of yours clear."

I've never fallen out of love.

"And when it's over? You won't prosecute Lola?"

"We have no reason to charge her with anything as of yet, especially if she cooperates with you. But we will need to interview her at length."

I think about what she's telling me. Think about how easy it will be to fall under the spell of the woman I once loved and still love a little too much. Could be that by entering into the FBI's little arrangement, I will be setting myself up for another fall. As Agent Crockett says, I'll just have to try my best to stay focused.

"One question: Why haven't you already picked up Clyne or Barter if you know where they're hiding out?"

Shaking her head.

"Can't take the chance that they'll destroy the flash drive. Far as we know, it's the only one in existence—though, of course, who knows how many times they've copied it. If they have, we'll have to deal with that when the time comes. We also don't know whom they've been in contact with since Barter came aboard, and whom they might lead us to. So our policy since we've located them has been to observe first and act later." Her hand on my thigh. "Now we have you and now we can act."

Sliding off the bed, she stands, slips into her skirt, and fixes it around her narrow waist.

I slide off the bed, wrap an arm around her, move in for a kiss. But she pushes me away.

"Fun's over, Romeo," she says. "You have homework to do. There are more items inside that bag that you'll need for the assignment. Go through it all and call me if you have any questions. I'll be available to you day and night. But call only if it's of the utmost importance. Got it? We don't want to risk a communications interception. My number is on the preset speed-dial list on the BlackBerry we included inside the bag."

Now fully dressed, she goes for the door. Before opening it, she turns back to me.

"Good luck, Moonlight. And be careful. Clyne and company have their fingers on some serious death and destruction. No telling what they're capable of when it comes to protecting it."

She lets herself out.

I step on over to the door, lock the deadbolt.

CHAPTER 13

I sit on the bed, naked, and smoke.

Not that I smoke a lot these days. The constriction of the blood vessels it causes inside my brain is not the safest thing in the world when you have a piece of .22 caliber hollow-point residing directly beside your cerebral cortex.

I should just quit outright.

But for some reason, I can't get myself to let go. As crazy as it seems, it's like letting go of the memory of Lola.

I set the laptop on my lap, feel the warmth from the processor against my bare thighs. I scroll through the photos of Clyne that are stored inside the Flickr account. Instead of the slightly overweight, whiskey-soaked, trench-coated APD detective, what we have now is a trim, concave-jawed, dressed-all-in-black phantom. In most of the shots, he's wearing narrow-framed sunglasses that succeed in hiding those sad eyes. Black turtleneck sweater, dark trousers, black jacket. Dressed just like I imagined a man to be hiding from international law to be dressed. In the shots, he's seated at a table in an outdoor café, sipping a cappuccino, a newspaper in his hands. Trim beard and shorter-than-short cropped hair on his head, both of which have been dyed black.

In a place like Albany, Clyne would stick out like a sore thumb among the pastel-clothed white-bread population. But not in Florence, where every other man or woman is dressed in dark clothing and looking European chic. Just like Lola appears in her photos. Long dark hair, tan face, black scarf wrapped around her neck. Barter is also dressed to blend. Dark suit and sunglasses, his goatee and mustache trimmed to precise specifications.

I go through all the pictures searching for anyone with whom the three might engage in conversation other than themselves. But all the shots are the same: Clyne, Lola, and Barter sitting at the table, drinking coffee, the men's faces painted with great expectations. As for Lola, her expression is always the same: one of doom.

I set the computer aside and pull the leather bag closer to me. Tip it upside down, the rest of its contents spilling out onto the bed.

There's a folded map of Florence. I unfold it. A few of the streets are highlighted in blaze yellow. One of the streets contains the guesthouse where I'll be staying. The second street shows the location of Harry's Bar. I guess the rest is up to me to figure out.

I set the map back down.

Next I pick up an envelope.

"Itinerary" is written on the outside in black Sharpie.

I open it, slide out the folded pages. I check out the electronic vouchers for the flights. Departure is at 6:00 p.m. tomorrow from JFK. Arrive in Frankfurt at 6:00 a.m. the next day. A quick flight over the Alps and I'm in Florence by 9:30 a.m. From there I'm to meet up with my contact, one Francesco Tasi, at a guesthouse called Il Ghiro, where I will be set up in a private room. Tasi will provide me with information when I get there. He will also outfit me with a weapon and ammunition. It's going to be one of those kinds of trips.

The bag has more goodies for me.

A modem for direct Internet communication with Agent Crockett and her gang. A small portable printer with fax and scanning capabilities. More credit cards besides the ones already stuffed into the wallet, including an AmEx and a Visa, both with $50K limits. Or so the Post-it notes stuck to them attest. There's also a debit card that accesses an ING cash account that contains a fifty-thousand-euro balance.

"Please hand in all receipts at the end of the project," insists yet another handwritten Post-it note attached to the debit card.

What else? Toothbrush, dental floss, toothpaste, deodorant, razors, shampoo—the whole kit and self-grooming caboodle.

And one more thing.

An additional bottle of Valium, to which Crockett has attached one more Post-it note with a hand-drawn smiley face on it.

I'm beginning to think she really likes me.

Later that night I dream: *I'm riding in a gondola with Lola. It's night, the black sky backlit with a full moon. We're somehow riding down the middle of Broadway in downtown Albany, the black crumbling macadam having given way to canals of gray-brown water. We're holding hands, listening to a song sung by the gondolier. It's sweet music by moonlight. Lola holds my hand tightly. She turns to me, kisses me. But then she pulls away, lets go of my hand. She says, "I can't do this." Lifting herself up, she jumps overboard and disappears into the lagoon, never to return...*

PART III

CHAPTER 14

Early Tuesday morning I land in Florence, Italy.

I'm groggy and disoriented from having self-medicated for the entire ten hours' worth of flying time. What can I say? Flying—the safest means of transportation there is—scares the living daylights out of me. Valium, ingested in the right amounts with the correct infusion of alcohol, will knock you out cold. Only when we started flying over the Alps did I wake up from the severe turbulence that occurs naturally from the up and down mountain drafts. So they tell me. Just the thought of kissing one of those beautiful white-capped summits head-on is enough to snap me out of a drug-induced near-death.

Standing outside the Santa Maria Novella train station where the airport cab has let me out, I check the map Crockett provided me back in New York. The guesthouse is only a few blocks away. Slinging my pack on my back, I wrap my leather carry-on around my shoulder and take a quick look around.

Florence.

Home of the Renaissance.

Home of Leonardo da Vinci.

Home of Dante and the *Divine Comedy* and all those levels of hell. Not that I remember much of it from my English and art history classes at Providence College. But this might be the perfect time to brush up.

I can't help but notice, coming and going from the marble-sided, art deco train station, dozens of the prettiest women I've ever seen. Many of them with long, flowing hair, and outfitted stylishly in short skirts, tall leather boots, and leather jackets to match. The way the language flows off their tongues as they speak to one another only enhances their attractiveness. So does the way they walk arm in arm, like lovers do in the States.

I shake the Valium fuzz from my brain and cross the busy street. I head down the Via Nazionale past the McDonald's and a Chinese restaurant toward the Via Faenza. The streets are narrow here, as are the sidewalks, which are full of people, young and old. Many of them look like natives, but there's a big Asian contingent here.

As I negotiate a space on the sidewalk, the Florence experience washes right back over me, like I never left here more than twenty years ago. Once again I'm exposed to that curious language mixture of Italian, Chinese, Japanese, and English. American English. Which makes sense, since there are so many American art schools in this town. What was it someone once said to me during my visit here right out of college? There are more Americans in Florence than Italians. Possibly. But this urban landscape, created from centuries-old stucco and stone buildings, their glass facades showing off fresh meats, cheeses, fruits, and wines—this place is all Tuscany. All Italian.

I move on past a two-man crew carrying a big gold-framed oil painting out through the open doorway of a townhouse toward a small, three-wheeled flatbed truck parked up on the slate-covered sidewalk. The men are smoking and yelling at one another.

I have no idea what they're saying, but it seems like their yells are in the normal course of their working relationship.

Up ahead of them, I spot some kids on motor scooters. Teenagers, riding white Vespas that look about as old as I am. The boys in skinny jeans drive while their miniskirted girlfriends press themselves up against their backsides, hanging on by wrapping their arms around their boyfriends' belted waists. As soon as the boys spot a couple of policemen on the corner, each of them shouldering automatic weapons, they slow down and pay attention to the road.

Farther up in the Piazza Santa Maria Novella resides a collection of beggars. One man with his right leg missing from the knee down. I see a woman dressed in a long, filthy dress and moth-eaten sweater, a kerchief covering her head. She's old, her face pockmarked with disease, age, and poverty. She holds an empty espresso coffee can out for the passersby to toss coins into. I make my way past them, until I come to something that sends a shiver up and down my spine. He's a man, but his limbs are so disjointed that his legs and knees are twisted one hundred and eighty degrees in the wrong direction, almost as if his hips were installed backward. He's got shoes on his hands and feet, and looks like a human who's been bred with a big dog or a small horse. With his inverted knees, he doesn't walk so much as he trots. In the cool, moist air, he's wearing only a T-shirt and cut-off jeans, and despite his condition, he's not a bad-looking guy of thirtysomething.

He catches my glance from just a couple of feet off the cobblestones. "*Ciao*," he greets. He's a got a small plastic bowl set in front of him. It's half-filled with coins.

"Hello," I say.

"You're American." He nods. "New York?"

"All from one word?" I say. "Yeah, you got it. Upstate. Albany."

He smiles, I smile. It's like we're two working-stiff strangers hitting it off at the local bar. You can spend a lifetime trying to connect with some people. Just ask my ex-wife, Lynn. But on some occasions, connecting can take only an instant. There's no explanation for it. Who knows, maybe this deformed man and I were friends in another life.

"Moonlight," I say. "Dick Moonlight."

"Carlo," he returns. "The magnificent half man, half animal. I was a superstar in the circus. But kids no more interested in the circus. Just Xbox and Wii."

I get it. I fish out a five-euro note from my pants pocket, drop it into his bucket.

"*Molto grazie*," he says, smiles. "Thank you, Moonlight."

I nod.

"Moonlight," he laughs. "Luna illuminata. Your name, *bellissimo*. Except for the Dick part."

"You had to say it, huh, Carlo?"

"*'Scuse*...could not help myself."

"I'm sure I'll see you around. You're a tough man to miss."

"You here on vacation? To see the Duomo?" He reaches back with his left hoof, or hand I should say, while balancing on the other. He sheds the shoe and reaches into the pocket of his cutoffs, comes back out with a business card, hands it to me.

I take it, give it a peek.

"Carlo the Great. Circus Actor and Tour Guide."

His cell phone number is located below that.

"Never seen a beggar who carries a business card," I say, pocketing the card.

"Tough times," he says, cocking his head. "You do what you have to do to survive."

I purse my lips. "I'll call if I need a guide."

"Call soon. I book up fast."

"I'd expect nothing less for a man of your talents," I say, and head on into the ancient city.

CHAPTER 15

The air is a combination of roast coffee, cooking meats and sauces, and even perfumes. The fact that the aromas combine with exhaust from the old cars and trucks does little to make it any less appetizing. Am I really here to steal back a flash drive for the FBI? Or was all that just a bad dream while I slept a Valium-induced sleep on the plane? A big part of me just wants to sit down at a café and drink espresso. Fuck the FBI.

Soon I find myself at the corner of Nazionale and Fienza. On the corner beside me, a coffee bar. Across the street from that, another coffee bar. Farther up ahead on the right, an old convent. The building I'm seeking, the Il Ghiro guesthouse, is located directly across from it.

I walk the stone street until I locate the building. I thumb the buzzer on the wall-mounted intercom and wait for a voice to emerge from the speaker.

"*Pronto*," says the tinny voice.

Facing the speaker, I say, "I'm looking for Francesco. He's expecting me."

"*Ahhh, si, si*," comes the happy voice. "Come in, yes, come in."

There's a loud buzz and click-clack sound of a mechanical bolt releasing, and the old heavy wood door opens on its own.

"All the way up, Mr. Moonlight," adds the voice.

I look directly up at a skylight through the center of a wraparound staircase constructed of marble treads and a brass banister.

"*Bella,*" I whisper to myself. I sound stupid trying to speak Italian.

"Welcome to Italy," echoes the voice from up on high.

I begin to climb six flights with a fifty-pound pack on my back and a leather shoulder bag filled with computer equipment. By the time I get to the top, what's left of my Valium haze has mostly been sweated out. As I catch my breath, a narrow blue door opens and out steps my contact.

Francesco.

"Welcome to Florence," says a forty-something, slim man dressed in Levi's and a pressed baby-blue button-down. "Shameful you are not here to see the museums and to soak in the culture."

"It's all cloak-and-dagger stuff from this point on," I say, nodding.

He tells me to come in.

I do it.

Behind me, the guesthouse door closes with a resounding slam. A heavy-duty deadbolt engages. Reminds me of a prison lockdown.

I follow Francesco down another narrow corridor to an open room that serves as his office. There's a desk that sits in front of a terrace and balcony separated from the interior with two slim french doors. The doors are open. Mounted on the plaster wall to my right is a giant map of Florence. Beside that, another giant map of the Italian boot. Beside that, a map of the globe.

Under the maps, running the length of the wall, is a counter that holds an automatic espresso machine. I begin to salivate just looking at it. Moonlight the exhausted.

To my left is a bathroom. Mounted to the wall above the bathroom door, a security camera. I look into the camera, and my contact notices me looking into it.

"Don't worry," he says. "It's not on right now."

"Why's it there, then?"

He cocks his head over his shoulder. "On occasion we have…let's call them 'guests'…who do not come as highly recommended as you."

I get the distinct feeling the FBI and Interpol are not this man's only clients.

We stand in weighted silence for a moment, until he suddenly holds out his hand. "But where are my manners?" he offers. "I am Francesco, owner of Il Ghiro. Do you know what Il Ghiro means, Mr. Moonlight?"

The only thing I feel more stupid at than trying to speak Italian is trying to translate it. I shake my head while setting my pack down against the map wall, but keeping the leather shoulder bag slung to my shoulder.

"It means to sleep like a church mouse," he goes on. "Or, in your case, to sleep like a church mouse while seeking out rats." He belly laughs and pats my back.

"Cloak and dagger," I repeat.

"But you must be tired. Would you like an espresso?"

I tell him I'd love one, or three. Is it possible we can mainline the caffeine directly into my veins?

"*Bene, bene.*"

He goes to the machine, sets a demi glass beneath the spot, and hits a red button on the side. Almost immediately a stream of steaming hot black coffee begins pouring into the cup. When it's through he hands the cup to me and fixes one for himself. There's a couple of wood stools set against the counter. He gestures for me to take a load off. Which I gladly do. Instead of seating himself behind the desk, he takes the other stool and sits.

For a brief moment we sit quietly and sip the hot coffee.

Then, after a couple more silent beats, he gets to it.

"As I am to understand, Mr. Moonlight," he says, "I will be providing you not only with lodging, but I will be your contact here for everything you need in support of your mission."

I drink down my coffee, feel the sudden but good caffeine rush. "You're aware of the details?"

"They tell me what I need to know. Such as, I know you are after a man, an American, who goes by the name of Dennis Clyne. Clyne possesses a data storage drive that contains information sensitive to the national security of the US and Europe, if not the world. Joining him in this venture is another man, an FBI man, by the name of Barter. Neither man has bothered to change his name, probably knowing that such a move is useless and very, how you say?"

"Cloak and dagger."

"*Si*, cloak and dagger." Then he says, "And joining Mr. Barter is—and this is difficult for me to say—your ex-lover, Dr. Lola Ross."

I feel the usual stomach drop when I hear her name spoken out loud.

He adds, "We have reason to believe Ross is being held against her will, in that she fears physical reprisal should she decide to leave Barter. It will be your job to infiltrate her world and get her to trust you with the location of the storage drive."

"Maybe I can get her to fall back in love with me while I'm at it."

"Ah yes," he says, his eyes lighting up.

"This is romantic Italy, am I right?"

"*Eco!*" he barks, patting my shoulder again. "I will help you with your love problem. In no time, Lola will be loving you again, Mr. Moonlight. But then, perhaps, that kind of love is already too broken for repair."

My stomach sinks some more.

"My immediate priority is to get my hands on that flash drive."

"I understand," he says, sliding off the stool. "Let's get started on it right away, shall we?"

He heads back behind his desk, opens the top right-hand drawer, pulls out an automatic. A .9 mm Walther PPK, along with two ammo clips filled with rounds, and its elastic shoulder holster. He sets the stuff down on the desk.

"I'm sure you're familiar with one of these?" he says.

"Yes, sir," I say. "James Bond's preferred choice of hand cannon."

"There will be considerable risk in this assignment. You must be cautious, vigilant."

"I used to be a cop," I reveal. "A New York cop. And truth be told, Francesco, someone's always taking a shot at me. So it seems."

He smiles. "Cloak and dagger," he repeats.

Cloak and fucking dagger.

CHAPTER 16

As I said, I've been to Florence before. Two decades, a wife, a life, an attempted suicide, and one beautiful little son ago. But Francesco is taking no chances. Together, we stand before the wall-mounted map of Florence. Using Il Ghiro as my benchmark, he employs his fingertip to trace the way to the Duomo and the large square it occupies. He also shows me the location of one of at least half a dozen cafés where Clyne, Barter, and Lola tend to spend a large part of their afternoons drinking coffee right out in the open like they haven't a care in the world, other than mingling with the tourists. He also points out Harry's Bar, which is located in a tall building not far from the banks of the Arno.

"Apparently, they feel they're invisible," I say.

"Or they are simply arrogant," Francesco points out in his perfect but Italian-accented English. "Clyne has his hands on the locations of a whole bunch of nukes and has devised a scheme to sell the information to the highest bidder, be it the Russian mob or perhaps a rogue terrorist organization. It's no coincidence that Barter has agreed to work with the former cop. It tells me it's quite possible that Barter was already in on the project in one form or another even before the data drive landed on European soil. An investor perhaps, or even a first-level player."

Francesco makes sense and I tell him so.

"*Si, si,*" agrees Francesco. "We might even suppose that, at this point, the only thing keeping Clyne alive is that he knows where the flash drive is hidden, and perhaps Barter does not. Or vice versa."

"That's definitely a possibility. You really think Lola could know of its location even if her boyfriend doesn't?"

He cocks his head, his eyes glued to the map and the small black ovular reproduction of the Duomo and the cathedral it covers.

"No, I do not," he tells me. "However, if you can perhaps find a way to get her to open up to you, she might be willing to help you find it. But she must feel she can trust you first."

I take hold of his forearm. I don't hold it tight, but I squeeze it just enough to get his attention. "I'm not about to place Lola in danger," I say. "No matter what, I still love her, and if what I'm about to do exposes her to danger in any way, I'll stop."

I release his arm.

"Remember, this is love and war we're dealing with, Mr. Moonlight," he explains, his brown eyes glued to mine. "And all is fair."

Francesco grabs my backpack. He leads me out of his office, down a narrow corridor, past the entrance doors, and finally to my room, the door of which is already open.

It's a large room with a tile floor and stucco walls, a cathedral ceiling with thick beams running across it and a *Casablanca* fan hanging down. In the center of the room is a double bed supported by a metal frame, and two wall-mounted sconces for light on either side. To the right of the bed is a small end table that supports a portable television, and beside it, a stand-alone closet. Behind the closet is the bathroom. Just a shower, sink, toilet, and bidet, not that I'll need it. On the far right of the bed is a desk pushed up against french windows that open onto the convent and, in the near distance, a view of Florence Cathedral's dome or Duomo, and far beyond that, the mountain town of Fesolie, which I visited during my last trip here. Spartan accommodations, but the perfect view. That is, if you were a honeymooner and in love.

Francesco sets down the pack against the bed. He suggests I take a rest. He gives me that look like a lot of people give me in Albany. The one that says, *"I'm aware of that piece of bullet in your head and the fact that you can buy the farm at any time."* I know the look very well by now. Behind the eyes is the sad knowledge that I somehow managed to survive my own suicide and that now I'm a head case who at times has trouble even trusting himself. After all, I've been known to forget things and my decision-making ability is not always the greatest, especially in times of great stress. I can also pass out without the slightest warning. So perhaps some rest is a good idea.

But I can't possibly rest.

My espresso-fueled adrenaline is flowing like electricity through hot wires, and I just got off a plane after almost a dozen hours cruising through the friendly skies. Nervous energy. Moonlight the wired.

Time to go to work.

An inventory of the things I need to carry on my person seems like it's in order. With Francesco standing beside me, I pull my passport from my pocket and set it on the bed. I do the same with my new mobile phone. I take the laptop computer and its power cord from the leather shoulder bag, set it onto the desk, open it, and begin booting it up. Then I pull out my wallet and set it on the bed beside the passport, the mobile smartphone, the Walther .9 mm, and one of the two extra ammo clips.

Taking a couple of steps back and away from the bed, I stare down at my weaponry and it feels considerably weak to me.

Turning to Francesco. "I'm prone to carry a small piece around my ankle as a backup," I tell him. "Would you be able to help out there?"

He nods, purses his lips. "I might have something you'll be interested in. If you'll excuse me." He exits the room and after a minute returns with a soft leather satchel. Loosening the straps on the satchel, he opens it to reveal a black-plated snub-nose .22 caliber five-shot Colt revolver, and along with it, a twelve-inch fighting knife I recognize as NATO-issue from my own days in the Persian Gulf War.

"Compliments of Il Ghiro," he says, exiting the room once more and returning with some duct tape. "Sadly, I have no holster for the .22. But I have plenty of tape for wrapping it around your leg. As for the knife, she can be fixed to your belt."

I reach out and gently pat him on the shoulder as a way of saying thanks.

"Just one more favor," I beg of Francesco. "Got a pencil I can borrow? And maybe a pad of paper or a notebook?"

"It's the simplest things that always go missing." He laughs. "We will have to remedy that." Once more he leaves the room and returns with a couple of sharpened pencils, which I stuff inside my leather shoulder bag along with the notebook. Slipping out of my jacket, I set it on the bed. I remove my shirt and toss it into the corner I'll designate for soiled laundry. Then, grabbing hold of the roll of duct tape, I set my left leg up on the bed. I pull up the cuff and cut off a piece of duct tape and tape the .22 to my left leg just above the boot top. Pull my pant cuff back over the pistol. Slide my foot off the bed and unbuckle my belt. I remove some of the narrow leather strap from the pant loops and slide on the knife sheath. Then I fish the strap back through the loops and once more buckle the belt.

I retrieve a clean white shirt from my pack and put it on, carefully buttoning it from bottom to top, leaving the neck open. I slip the elastic shoulder holster over my head and shoulders, adjusting it to fit comfortably. Slipping back into my leather coat, I store my passport in an inside pocket along with my billfold. I place the mobile phone into the second interior pocket and store one of the extra ammo clips in the left-hand pocket.

Easy access.

Picking up the .9 mm and the second clip from off the bed, I slap the clip home and cock a round into the chamber. Thumbing the safety on, I drop the piece, grip inverted, into the holster. I slip the shoulder bag over my head and allow it to hang against my left shoulder and my right hip. That way it won't get in the way if I have to make a quick play for the Walther.

When I slide on a pair of Ray-Ban aviator sunglasses, I know I'm finally locked and loaded.

When we exit the room something dawns on me.

"How about a key?" I say.

Francesco reaches into his pocket, hands me a skeleton key.

"You're kidding," I say, taking the key in hand and locking the door. "I haven't seen one of these since my grandmother was still alive."

"Don't worry," he assures me. "You are my only guest until this little issue of the data drive recovery is behind us and perhaps, just perhaps, you will have your Lola back, safe and sound."

In my head I see Lola's big brown eyes, rich olive-skinned face, thick heart-shaped lips, and long, lush, brunette hair. Then I picture her being made to share Special Agent Christian Barter's bed every night. My stomach caves in on itself and my breathing becomes slightly strained.

Keep a clear head, Moonlight. Don't let emotions get in the way of your job.

Francesco approaches the door that leads out to the stairs, releases the deadbolt. "Don't take on too much this afternoon," he warns. "Reacquaint yourself with the city. Time is of the essence, but we still have enough time to enact our plan."

I feel the solid weight of the pistol against my ribs. "I promise not to make a mess of things," I say. "Yet."

"Your reputation precedes you." He laughs.

"That bad, huh?" I say, and begin the long descent down six flights of stairs.

CHAPTER 17

I make a check on the time.

Seems like it could be late afternoon. But it's only ten forty-five in the morning. Italy at this time of year is six hours ahead of the States, and already I'm beginning to feel the effects of jet lag.

It will only get worse.

The cure?

Coffee. Good, strong Italian espresso.

Out the door of the building I hook a right and follow the narrow cobbled street toward the four corners. All around me fashionably dressed young people are hurrying to and from their art classes, while busy working people go about their lives in the many shops and eateries I pass by.

I cross the Nazionale and continue down Fienza just like Francesco instructed and proceed to the left before coming to a fork in the road at a local branch bank. When I get to the end of this short stretch of road, I take yet another left and lose my breath at the vision before me.

It's a tidal wave of white marble accented in green and red lines. I move toward the tidal wave until the road ends and I enter a square that's dominated by the Florence Cathedral and its massive dome, or Duomo. How builders were able to construct this marble immensity six hundred years ago is an absolute mystery to me. But just looking up at it from down inside the cobbled square, I can't help but feel somehow small and insignificant. And maybe I am.

I decide to take a brisk walk around the entire cathedral, stopping only long enough to get a better look at a detail or a bronze door or at the tourists who have climbed the interior stairs and now occupy the cupola and gaze down upon me from hundreds of feet up. Not a happy place for those people who have a fear of heights or, like me, a sudden and uncontrollable habit of passing out when they least expect it. The structure is so large it takes me ten minutes to walk around the entire perimeter.

My mortician dad used to purchase headstones from the Italian marble craftsman in downtown Albany. "Leave it to the Italians to build something that lasts and lasts," he'd always say. "And believe me, Richard, death lasts a real long time."

Back where I started.

I take my first good look at the many cafés that border the Duomo square. All of them are filled with patrons. Tourists, mostly.

I try to take a close look at the people who occupy the tables and chairs in the outdoor seating areas. But not too closely. The sunglasses help. As I casually stroll past the establishments, I don't see anyone I recognize. No Clyne, Barter, or Lola. You'd think with all the surveillance the FBI and Interpol have been maintaining on my three amigos, we'd have established which café they hang out at most often. But therein lies the problem. The three amigos don't frequent one single café for very long. Rather, they tend to switch up a lot. Let's face it, Barter isn't stupid. Of all people he would know that he's being watched. Wasn't that long ago that he was still under federal employ to be a watcher himself.

It's time to plant myself.

But I need to find a place that will give me a bird's-eye view of the square. I settle on an empty table set directly in front of the cathedral's marble steps. I pull out the paper and pencil that Francesco provided for me earlier and pretend to take on the guise of a poet who has come here for inspiration and luck.

The ruse works too.

Better than I thought it would.

Because I haven't even written down my first word yet when I recognize the voice of my ex-lover.

CHAPTER 18

I'm careful not to look directly in the direction of her voice.

Seated at the small table, pencil pressed to paper, I manage to sneak a peek over my left shoulder. I see three people. Two men walking side by side and a woman lagging a step or two behind.

Lola.

Like the men, she's dressed in black.

Leather boots that rise up to her knees, black jacket over turtleneck sweater. She's wearing black-rimmed Jackie O's over her eyes. The men wear black leather jackets over dark trousers and black shoes. They too wear sunglasses. Clyne the larger. Barter the smaller, but wiry and in cross-trainer shape.

As they pass, I'm able to look directly at their backs. I'm resisting the almost irresistible urge to run up behind them and scream, "Guess who!"

Then I might simply pull out the .9 mm, hold it on the two big boys point-blank while I demand return of the flash drive I'd stupidly handed to Clyne in the first place, all those months ago when my heart was bleeding for the lonely, newly divorced cop. At the same time I could grab hold of Lola, pull her to me, press the pistol barrel against her right temple, scream something over-the-top dramatic like, "Hand over the flash drive or the girl gets it!"

But that would just blow the entire mission. It might also get me and Lola killed, or at the very least, arrested by the Italian police while Clyne and Barter make their escape.

Best to stick to the plan.

I pack up the pencil and paper and begin to follow the three-some. From a distance.

I maintain a separation of forty or fifty feet between them and me as we walk across the square to a road that runs perpendicular to the Duomo square. The road is wider than some of the other roadways in the city. We pass an open area that's home to a large five-star hotel on the left and a cobbled square that sports a couple of expensive cafés along with a brass band and an old-fashioned carousel of colorful wooden horses, tigers, and lions. My ten-year-old boy, Harrison, would have loved that carousel back when he was a toddler. Christ, he'd still love it. I wonder if he gets to ride carousels in sunny LA?

Up ahead is a series of expensive clothing shops on both sides of the streets. Renaissance-era structures of brick, wood, and tile, now retrofitted with big glass storefront windows bearing the names Chanel, Gap, Prada, Old Navy, and so on. There's even a Hard Rock Café in Florence now. I might as well be back in Albany at the mall. But then, I don't go to the mall.

Not far up ahead, the Ponte Vecchio and its many jewelry shops. The street used to house butcher shops, which made sense, since the butchers could simply toss the discarded bloody carcasses through the openings in the floor and into the river. When they had to relieve themselves, that would go into the

Arno too. The residents of this town might have been smart enough to initiate the modern era of architecture, literature, and art, but they didn't know enough not to drink the putrid river water. Many of them nearly died in a typhoid epidemic of 1696. Necessity might be the mother of invention, but so is protracted death.

For a moment, I think the three amigos might head on to the bridge, but instead they hook a left down a narrow alley located directly across from the open-air leather market. I keep my distance as they come out upon another major square, this one housing the giant marble Poseidon and the near-perfect replica of Michelangelo's *David* that stands guard outside the Palazzo Vecchio entrance. I feel my pulse elevate at the sight of these statues, just like I did when I first laid eyes on them as a kid soon after my mother died, and again later as a slightly-drunk-on-Chianti young adult. But it elevates more when Lola and her companions stop outside one of the half dozen open-air cafés and seat themselves at a table that overlooks the entire square.

I see that there's another café right beside theirs, and I take a table that allows me a clear and unobstructed view of their table. I order a tall beer from the neatly dressed waiter. When the beer arrives, along with a small plate of green olives soaked in olive oil and fresh ground pepper, I once more pull out the pencil and paper, settle in for a quiet afternoon of observing my ex-lover and the men who are holding her against her will in a foreign land.

CHAPTER 19

They order drinks. Or the men order drinks. Beers.

Lola orders a coffee.

When it comes, she simply stares down into it, as if the dark, frothy vision is her only means of escape.

The men talk. I have no idea what they're saying. Discussing their next move? Or, more likely, just shooting the shit while they wait for a potential buyer. Stands to reason that they're remaining in Florence for as long as they have for one reason and one reason only: to meet a buyer. But I can bet the title to Dad's pride-and-joy 1978 Cadillac funeral hearse that said buyers haven't arranged a specific time to meet them. Not yet, anyway. They've merely told them where they will meet them, and to be in that exact place every day at a specific time. Only when the buyers are ready—if they're ever ready—will they then come to the sellers.

It's the only explanation for their taking the chance on staying in the same city for as long as they have, knowing they're being watched by both the good guys and a variety of bad guys. Stands to reason that today's choice of café isn't indiscriminate either. My guess is that they were instructed to make this move. And if that's the case, the potential buyers are probably getting closer to meeting their sellers and making a deal.

I'm familiar with this kind of thing from my days in the APD. Drug dealers use the wait-and-observe tactic all the time. They ask a potential client to meet them at a specific place. But they don't offer up a specific time of the meet. For two good reasons. It gives the buyer a chance to spy on the would-be client, make sure they're not the police in disguise. And two, constantly showing up every day, day after day, displays serious intention on the part of the client. Means they're not about to jerk the buyer's chain and waste his or her time. If one were to require a third reason for making their seller wait, it would be to make certain that the buyer isn't about to walk into an ambush. Conversely, it allows for the buyer to at least prepare for the worst should a buy go bad. That is, if the lead starts to fly, the buyer will already have his gunners and sharpshooters in place in and around the square, from the windows and rooftops.

Something happens.

Lola says something to the men. Whatever she says causes Barter to lean in tight to her, his mouth so close to her face she can probably smell his halitosis. He clamps his hand around hers on the table and says something back. Something with a little heat sprinkled on top. She yanks her hand away. Hard. I hear the distinct cry of "Go! To! Hell!"

He tries to grab her hand again.

It's all I can do to remain seated and anonymous. But I have no choice.

Lola, however, gets up from the table.

She walks away.

Barter starts to laugh. "Don't get lost, Lo!" he barks. "I might not see you with my eyes. But I fucking see you, all right."

She raises up her right hand, flips him off over her shoulder.

Fuck you, Barter.

I couldn't agree more.

CHAPTER 20

Lola is going to pass my table, within three feet of where I'm sitting.

As if it were scripted this way. The perfect time to get reacquainted. I make certain she sees my face by raising up my aviators.

She stops dead in her tracks.

Stares at me.

Her mouth hangs open.

"Just keep walking," I tell her. "Around the corner."

She walks on. I give her a long minute or so while my stomach muscles tighten and I lose all the moisture in my mouth. Then I follow.

She's waiting for me across the street and a few doors down, in a shop doorway. I cross to her.

I know her so well. Her touch, her smell, her taste. But I have no idea who this woman before me is. I only know that I love her. No matter what's happened these past few months. I still love her.

"How are you, Lola?" I say.

She steals a quick gaze over my shoulder. The color has drained from her face. She drills her eyes into me. "You shouldn't be here, Richard," she warns. "It's not safe."

"Look who's talking," I say. "Word up is that the relationship isn't working out."

She works up a hint of a smile, despite the shock of running into me here in Florence of all the places on God's earth.

"Do you know where Harry's Bar is?"

"I know it. It's across from the Vespucci bridge."

"Meet me there tomorrow, five o'clock. Please don't try to contact me until then."

"I'll be there," I assure her.

"Get away from here as soon as I'm gone," she insists. "They see you, they will kill you."

She steals another anxious glance over her shoulder, as if she can see Barter and Clyne from where we're standing.

"Tomorrow," she says, turning back to me.

And then she's gone.

CHAPTER 21

I pass by the square on my way back to the guesthouse. Clyne and Barter are still sitting at the table, making small talk, obviously waiting for someone to show who seems not to be showing. I see their faces as I pass them by, but it's Lola's face that's implanted in my head directly beside that hollow-point bullet fragment. My heart is beating so fast, I feel like I might pass out. Not an unusual situation for me even during the best, most stress free of times.

Heading back toward Il Ghiro, I can't help but feel lighter than air on one hand and full of fear on the other.

I'm meeting Lola for a drink tomorrow.

If I want to recover that flash drive, and if I want to stay out of prison, and if I want my IRS problem to go away, I have to make her trust me. If I want to rescue her from Barter, I'll have to steal her away. I have a job to do, and I have a broken heart that's bleeding all over again at the sight of Lola.

That night I lie in bed staring at the plaster ceiling and at the *Casablanca* fan, its wide metal blades spinning slowly around, circulating the warm, humid air. Outside the open french windows, people walk past, the soles of their shoes clapping against the cobbles, their liquor- and wine-soaked laughs bouncing off the four-hundred-year-old plaster and brick walls.

I lie naked, smoking a cigarette, the cloud of blue smoke rising up to the spinning fan blades. I'm here to do a job. No, correction—I'm here to right a wrong that's all my fault. Funny that it should take a head case like me to start this trouble, and now to end it. But I can't do it without Lola's help. I can only hope she will trust me enough to reveal the location of the flash drive. Assuming she knows of its location. Only when that happens will I have the upper hand and the business of separating Lola from Barter and Clyne can begin.

I smoke the last of the cigarette, crush it out in the ashtray set beside the bed. Listening to the occasional man or woman pass by my window on the cobbled street below, I feel a slight breeze entering in through the open window. My mind drifts off. I'm not asleep, exactly, but I'm not fully awake either, as the events that came to shape my life and death almost one year ago replay themselves in my head…

I'm lying on my back inside a narrow downtown Albany alley.

Three faces stare down at me. All the same face. The face of the president. President Obama. He always seemed like such a nice guy to me. Way too nice for the office. But now here are three nice-guy presidents kicking me in the ribs, kidneys, and stomach with their steel-toed boot tips. One of them kicks me in the face, loosens my back teeth. The one in the middle steps away, presses a handheld voice synthesizer to his throat, tells me, "You should have stayed away from Peter Czech!"

Then I'm floating above a bed inside the Albany Medical Center ICU. My sig other Lola is standing by my side looking sad and forlorn at the death of her boyfriend, but also looking choice in tight white jeans and a silk black blouse, Jackie O sunglasses covering tear-swelled eyes and long, lush dark hair draping her chiseled face. I'm sad for her on one hand, but on the other, it lightens the heart to know that Lola is true blue. That she is standing by my side even in death.

But then something happens.

A man enters the room.

Some young guy.

He brushes up against her, runs his right hand over her ass. It almost looks like they're about to make out over my dead body.

Suddenly I'm trying to jump back into my beat-up body. Suddenly I want my life back so I can beat the life out of Some Young Guy...

The scene shifts. But the setting remains the same—the hospital room, me in the bed. I'm alive again. Barely. Lola and Some Young Guy are gone. But the Obama-masked men are back. They surround my hospital bed. The one on my left is jabbing me with a scalpel. He's using the sharp tip to pry out one of my surgical staples. The pain is so intense, I see red.

"Where is fleshy box?" the chief Obama standing at the foot of the bed demands in a Russian-accented voice.

"I. Don't. Know," I choke out.

I feel the flick of the scalpel once more, and then POP goes the staple.

I hear the ping of the steel staple hitting the hard floor. Then I pass out...

The scene shifts once more to the top floor of the old Montgomery Ward building in North Albany. The space is big and wide, like the giant warehouse it once was. Set in the middle of the big room is a room within a room: a room created out of translucent plastic, with an attached ventilation and respiration system. An operating room.

On the operating table, facedown, is Peter Czech. There's a team of doctors working on him. Standing off to the side is Lola and Some Young Guy, who, it turns out, is really not so young after all. His *name is Christian Barter, and he's an agent for the FBI. He and Lola are the biological childhood parents of Peter Czech, and now that they have found their long-lost son in adulthood, they have also rediscovered one another.*

Suddenly a commotion coming from the operating table and the alarm of a flatlined heart. Lights flash on and off, buzzers buzz, and bells chime. The doctors toss down their scalpels and suction tubes. They rip off their masks.

"He's dead," they lament to Lola. "We are so very sorry. But your son, he is dead."

Lola bursts into tears, presses her face into Barter's chest...

And now I'm awake. Which means I must have drifted off to sleep, however briefly, my vivid memories coming at me in the form of an accurate dream.

But here's the thing: I'm definitely not dreaming anymore because I'm definitely not sleeping. I have opened my eyes, and all I see is President Barack Hussein Obama standing over me.

Correction—three President Obamas are standing over me.

Two of the Obamas stand on either side of me. They each hold automatics, the barrels of which are pressed against each of my temples. I wonder if they realize that if they shoot at the same time, they'll blow my brains out, but they'll also shoot each other. Would serve the fuckers right.

The middle Obama backs away, goes to the window, looks out. He walks with a severe limp, like he has a fake leg. When he returns to the bed, he reaches inside his black leather jacket, pulls out his own automatic. He jabs the barrel into my left kneecap. The pain makes me jump.

"You like your knees, don't you, motherfucker?"

He speaks English with a heavy Russian accent. Unlike the Obamas who killed me in the States, these guys don't use voice synthesizers to hide the fact that they're Russians. I hate Russians. Correction—I hate Russian mobsters. But it's OK. They hate me too.

"Speak up, little bitch!" he demands, jamming the barrel into my knee.

"Yes, I do!" I bark. "I like my knees!"

He pulls his gun away, unbuckles his belt, and allows his trousers to drop. Besides the fact that I can't help but notice his choice of Eurotrash man-thong for undergarments, I can see in the half-light of the room that there's a huge divot in his left leg where I shot his kneecap off point-blank nearly a year ago. Back when I was in search of the same flash drive I'm in search of now. But for different reasons.

"Boris," I say.

"It is not Boris, Yankee Doodle fuck!" he snaps. "It is Gregor. Russian Boris is only in American movies. *Red Dawn* or *Red Sonja* starring the great Bruce Willis."

"Arnold is in *Red Sonja*," corrects the Russian Obama to my right. "Bruce Willis is *Die Hard*."

"What-the-fuck-ever," says Gregor. "Do not correct me when I am working." He hoists up his pants again, pulls back the hammer on the piece, and trains it point-blank on my knee. "Now, Mr. Moonlight, I am prepared to blow both your knees off as repayment for what you have done to me back in that stench hole, Albany. But first I need you to locate my fleshy drive. Do we have understanding?"

"What fleshy drive? I don't have it, remember? The police have it."

Gregor nods at the Russian Obama on my left. He holsters his piece, takes hold of my left hand, jams it down flat on the mattress. The Obama on my right raises up his knee, jams it down onto my shoulder, pinning me to the bed.

I begin to squirm, until Gregor shifts his pistol barrel from my left kneecap to my pride-and-joy golden jewels.

"Show Mr. Moonlight how serious we are this time about fleshy box!"

The Obama on my left pulls out a bowie knife the size of the Italian boot. He positions the very tip of my left pinky at the bottom of the long, chrome-plated blade. He presses it in tight.

I'm squirming again, but the Russian pinning me down is a giant of a man. He's as big as a pro football player. Bigger maybe. Both goons are huge. I have nowhere to go.

I feel the blade press against my pinky. Feel the blade enter. Feel the burn of blade and flesh and spurting blood. Feel the blade against bone. Then, with one quick downward slice of the knife, I feel the tip of my pinky separate from the finger just above the knuckle.

I try to scream. But the air is sucked from my lungs.

The real pain hasn't registered yet. Nor will it for a few seconds.

Gregor looks around the room, locates a T-shirt. He knows what's coming. He shoves the shirt into my gaping mouth.

That's when the burning electric pain hits like Mount Vesuvius erupting with burning hot ash over Pompeii.

This time when I try to scream, the T-shirt gags me.

Blood is pumping out of my pinky. What's left of it.

The Obama with the knife steps back. They all step back.

"I will check on you from time to time, Mr. Moonlight," says Gregor. "Each time you do not have fleshy box, I will remove a piece of your body. Do we make ourselves perfectly cruel?"

The big Obama clears his throat. "You mean *clear*. Do we make ourselves *clear*?"

Boris turns, shoots a sour look at the big-ass Obama. "Don't you interrupt me, big stupid fuck of a man." Then back at me. "Are we clear, Moonlight?"

I'm holding my left hand in my right hand. I pull the T-shirt out of my mouth and jam it onto the bleeding stub.

"Fuck, fuck, fuck…"

"Are we clear!" Gregor shouts again.

"Yeah, clear," I moan.

With that, the Obamas leave the room, closing the door behind them.

Fucking cruel Russians.

CHAPTER 22

I feel the T-shirt filling with blood. I need a hospital, but I can't risk blowing my cover. Maybe I should call Francesco. Maybe he'll know what to do. Or maybe he's working with the Russians. Fucked if I know what to do. I'm bleeding. I'm badly cut. I let the injury go, I risk gangrene by first light. I risk losing my entire hand. I happen to like my hand. Francesco is the only one who can possibly help me. I decide to take a chance on calling him.

I fumble for the cell on the nightstand.

But before I can grab it, I hear the sound of footsteps climbing the six flights of stairs that lead to the top floor of the guesthouse. I pull my piece out from under the mattress, where I placed it for easy access before getting into bed, just in case some Russian goons might pull a B and E and torture me. Go figure.

The footsteps stop.

The guesthouse door at the top of the stairs opens.

I thumb back the pistol hammer.

This time I'll shoot at whatever moves in the dark.

Ask questions later.

CHAPTER 23

The guesthouse door slams shut.

Running. Down the narrow corridor.

The door to my room flies open.

"Ricardo!"

Francesco enters.

My host is eyeing an empty bed. An empty bed with blood on it. My blood.

My. Fucking. Blood.

Francesco takes a step forward. A slow step, like he senses an ambush.

He should sense an ambush.

I press the barrel of the Walther up against the back of his head with my good hand, my bad hand pressed between my naked thighs.

"Down," I say, through clenched teeth. Grinding teeth. "Down on the fucking floor. Now. Down. Now."

Francesco raises up his hands like he knows the protocol. Slowly he descends.

"I am too late to save you," he says, his voice an octave higher than I remember it from this morning.

I cock back the hammer.

"You, Francesco," I say. "How do you say double-cross in Italian?"

"It is not like you think. It is truly—"

"Let's see, cross is *croce*, right?"

"Please take the gun away, Ricardo."

"*Croce*, am I right, you fuck? Am. I. Right?"

"*Sì, sì.* Yes, you are right."

"And double is *dople* or something like that. Tell me! Tell! Me!"

"*Doppia.*"

"Say it all. No wait. Say 'I am a bad *doppia croce*.'"

"It is not...I am not...."

"Turn around."

"'*Scuse?*"

"Turn around! On your knees!"

He does it.

I press against his nose. Not directly on the nose, but on the side, his left nostril pressed in like an almost-flat bicycle tire.

"Say it. Now. Say it or I blow your nose off. That would be better than killing you. I lost a finger and now you can lose a nose and then we're even. Say! It!"

He releases a breath while I press the gun even harder against his nose. So hard a tear falls from his left eye. He clears his throat. "I. Am. A. *Doppia. Croce.*"

"Again. Faster."

"I am a *doppia croce.*"

"Again...faster."

"I am a *doppia croce.*"

"Faster, louder."

"IAMADOPPIACROCE!!"

I see the elbow fly into my crotch before I feel a pain that only God Himself could have personally designed—on the eighth day, when He invented torture.

I drop the gun.

I drop the blood-soaked T-shirt.

I drop myself onto the floor and assume the fetal position on my right side.

Francesco picks up the Walther, aims it at me.

I manage the strength necessary to make a pistol with my injured hand. I point my extended index finger at my left temple.

"Shoot. Me," I say. "Shoot. Me. Dead. Now."

My hand falls. My balls inflate and pulsate with gut-tearing excruciation.

And then, by the grace of God, I pass out.

When I come to I'm back on the bed. The pain in my balls has receded, giving way to more pain in my left hand. My Walther is resting on the nightstand beside the bed. My initial instinct is to go for it. But just the sight of Francesco standing at the end of the bed, his arms crossed over his chest, his face radiating tight-jowled annoyance tells me maybe I was all wrong. Maybe my host isn't a double-crosser after all. A *doppia croce*. Maybe, just maybe, he was trying to tell the truth.

"I saw the three men leave the building over the security system. It was too late by then. My apologies for not paying better attention, but such is the nature of my business. I am only one man."

"We're on camera? Even in here?"

He makes a sweeping gesture with this open right hand. "Look around you. You can't see me, but I can see you."

"How the fuck could they have gotten in?"

"Any number of ways. My guess, Ricardo?"

"Try me."

"More than likely, they waited for the meter man to make his rounds. He comes every Monday afternoon. They simply walk in behind him, when the front door to the building is opened."

"OK, but how about getting through that prison lockdown of a door out front? How did they get the four-digit code?"

He shakes his head. "I have no answer for the code, but it is not impossible to discover it, with the right inside connections. As far as the lock is concerned, it must have been picked." He holds up his skeleton key. "Perhaps it's time for a better security system."

We both stare down at my injured hand, now wrapped back up in the bloody T-shirt.

"Again," he says after a time, "I can only offer you my sincerest apology. I must ask you to dig deeper as well and to trust me."

I look at him. His wide brown eyes, his slim build, his thick black hair. He seems like a very nice guy. Someone I would gladly share a beer with in different circumstances.

"OK," I say. "But from now on, I want you here at all times. OK?"

He nods. "Agreed."

"I need a hospital," I say, my left hand trembling under the T-shirt. I can feel the clipped finger curled into itself like a frightened caterpillar.

Francesco flips on the overhead. The light stings my eyes, adding to my collection of bodily pain.

I remove the T-shirt, expose the bloody tip of a finger.

"They did this to me. Those fucking Obamas."

"Obamas. Like the president. I saw their masks on the monitor."

He sits down, holds out his hands like he wants to examine my wound. "May I?"

Fucker throbs and stings. But I nod OK.

He gently takes hold of my forearm, peels back the pinky finger. The sting shoots electric up my arm into my neck.

"Knife?"

"Big one," I say.

He cocks his head. "It's not all bad. The fingertip is still there. But he gave you a very deep cut. I will fix it, however."

"You?"

"Stay where you are," he says, getting up, heading out of the room and into his office. "I hope you don't mind the feel of needle and thread."

"Love it," I say. "Compared to your elbow slamming into my balls."

He comes back in with a small tray. There's a surgical needle wrapped in clear plastic and a spool of medical thread also wrapped in plastic. A bottle of rubbing alcohol occupies the tray beside a bottle of Betadine ointment, along with a fistful of cotton balls. Aside from that, the tray also sports a syringe that's been locked and loaded with something, and one more thing: a drinking glass half full of an amber-colored liquid. Something tells me Francesco has seen his share of wounds before.

"Drink this," he says like an order, handing me the drinking glass. "It's American whiskey. Jack Daniels. Your brand, I believe."

"You shouldn't have, Francesco," I say, holding the warm glass in my right hand. "Fuck that. Yes, you damn well should have." Then I add, "Salute!" and down the entire two shots.

Setting the glass back onto the tray, I feel the calming warmth of the whiskey enter into my system. Meanwhile, Francesco takes hold of the syringe with his fingertips, takes aim with the needle tip.

"I don't have to tell you this is not going to be a pleasant experience."

"Just...you know...do it. Do. It."

He pushes the needle into my finger. The sting shoots up the nerve canal, all the way up my arm, into my neck and head. It brings tears to my eyes.

"This is a cocktail of antibiotic and tetanus," he informs. "One can never be too careful in these matters, my friend."

The memory of my holding a gun against his nose only fifteen or so minutes ago flashes through my brain. Now I'm allowing him to inject me with some chemical concoction. For all I know, I'll be paralyzed within a few seconds or just plain dead. But then, what choice do I have? I need this man more than he needs me. It's a matter of trust or faith. How did my dad describe faith whenever he'd console one of his numerous grieving customers? It's about believing in something you can't see, hear, or feel. In this case, my faith in Francesco is more than that. It's now an official leap of faith.

The needle extracted, I wipe my eyes with the back of my uninjured hand.

"These Russian fellows," he goes on, "they want the same thing you want? What you have been sent here for?" He's asking the right questions, but I'm sure he already knows the answers.

I nod while he pats at the wound with an alcohol-soaked cotton ball.

I cringe at the sting, but it's not quite as bad as having that three-inch-long needle impaled in my flesh.

"Please be still," he adds.

"Yes, the Russians want what I want. Always have."

"They are from the Russian government. Mr. Medvedev's government. Or should I say Mr. Putin's?"

More patting on the wound.

"Jeez, you done there, Francesco? This is worse torture than the Russians'. Worse than your bony elbow."

He giggles, pulls away the cotton ball. "But of course," he says.

I take a quick glance at the finger. The blood is all gone. But Francesco is getting ready to apply the first stitch. He looks at me looking at him and the finger.

"This is going to sting. Again."

"Got any more whiskey?"

He retrieves another two fingers for me, which I immediately shoot.

"You should refrain from too much alcohol while on duty," he suggests.

"Never thought about it like that," I say, once more setting the empty glass onto the tray. "On duty with the FBI in order to save my ex-girlfriend. Save the world. Save my ass."

"Yes, it all sounds very strange, doesn't it, Ricardo."

He tells me to set my palm down flat onto the table. Taking firm hold of my damaged pinky finger, he prepares to enter the needle and stitch.

"I don't have to tell you about the hurt," he whispers before beginning, echoing his previous warnings.

"You are one painful son of bitch, Francesco," I say. "Anyone ever tell you that?"

He smirks.

"Yes," he says. "My ex-wife used to say something like that all the time."

He presses the needle deep.

"She was right," I say and exhale. "So. Fucking. Right."

CHAPTER 24

When I'm sufficiently sewed back up, Francesco packs up the soiled medical waste, sets it onto the tray, puts it aside.

"Try to stay off the finger for a few days," he says, beaming.

I say nothing while the pinky tip throbs.

"That's a joke," he adds. "Get it? Stay off the finger."

"Your English is excellent," I say. "I don't pick my nose with that digit anyway."

Laughing, the guesthouse owner exits the room and comes back in a few minutes with a bottle. The Jack. I guess he's decided that we might as well get drunk. Damn the danger that lurks right outside these walls in the form of Obama-masked Russian thugs.

"I had been saving this bottle as a surprise for you when your mission was accomplished. But now that you have been injured in the line of duty, I see no reason to hold back any further."

He pours us each a small glass. He hands me mine.

I raise it up to him. "For tomorrow we die," I toast.

"You mustn't talk like that." He winks, sipping his whiskey. His eyes light up as he adds, "Strong. But sweet."

"I just think of it as sweet," I say, downing my third drink of the night.

He looks at me with a curious expression before shooting his.

He fills two more glasses.

"We'll let these sit," I tell him.

He nods, relieved.

"Were you able to spot the two men who possess the flash drive?"

"In the Palazzo Vecchio. They seemed to be waiting for someone. And waiting."

"A buyer perhaps. That has been our information. Iranian most likely. Florence is full of Iranians. All the street vendors are Iranian. Perhaps I can arrange for you to talk with someone who can help. He sells leather goods in the San Lorenzo market."

"He sells other things too, I'm guessing," I say, taking another small sip of the newly poured whiskey.

"Indeed he does. If there are interested buyers in the flash drive, it's possible he will know who they are and if they are serious and perhaps, just perhaps, when they might show up to make the purchase. That's when you might make your move to intercept the goods."

"I'm hoping it doesn't get to that, Francesco."

"I'm sorry. I do not understand."

"I spoke with Lola yesterday. We spotted one another as she angrily walked away from the café table where Clyne and Barter were sitting, perhaps waiting for their elusive Iranian buyer."

He drinks. "She recognized you, then."

"Of course. But at first she didn't want to believe it was me. Or so I suspect, my friend."

"I see."

"She knows why I'm here and what I have to do."

"Will she help you?"

"She's being kept here against her will. She knows she made a mistake in trusting her ex-lover. She will help me. Tomorrow I'm to meet her at Harry's Bar on the river."

"She will take you to the flash drive?"

"That's what I'm hoping. It's possible this could be over in twenty-four hours, and Lola and I will be on a plane out of here before midnight strikes tomorrow night."

Francesco reaches into his pocket, pulls out a small notebook, writes something down on a piece of paper, tears it off, hands it to me.

"What's this?"

"It's the name and stall number of the man who might give you information regarding the possible Iranian buyers. You should at least speak with him and find out when a drop might take place. Your FBI might be very interested in who the players are. To discover their identity would be a feather in your hat."

"I just told you, I'm meeting Lola tomorrow evening. And it's 'feather in your cap.'"

He finishes his drink. "Mr. Moonlight," he says, "we have a saying in Italy: if something looks too easy, it is likely to be impossibly difficult."

I feel my built-in shit detector poking at the insides of my stomach. Somehow I know for certain that Francesco is right.

I say, "It's possible, or maybe even likely, that Clyne and Barter have not revealed the location of the flash drive to Lola."

He cocks his head over his right shoulder. "A valid assumption." He goes for the door. "See the man in the market tomorrow. At the very least he will give you information, which in itself might lead you to the flash drive, inevitably. And, Mr.

Moonlight…" He allows his thought to drift off, like he's hesitant to share it for fear of reprisal.

"What is it?"

"We have another saying in Italy you might like to know."

"What is it?"

"Be careful which head you make your decisions with."

I can't help but smile. "We have that same saying in the US. Or a version thereof."

"Then you understand my meaning very clearly."

Lola. Me. Us. My obsession.

"I will meet the man in the market. First thing in the morning."

"Prudent of you."

He goes to leave and retire to his quarters down the hall. Or so I assume.

"Francesco," I call out.

He turns to face me.

"This man," I say, "he can be trusted? I'm not walking into a trap, I pray."

He bites down on his bottom lip. "Never trust a soul, Mr. Moonlight," he warns. "Not even your own."

He exits my room without taking the whiskey bottle with him.

CHAPTER 25

With my entire left hand throbbing and my midsection still tender, I don't have a chance in hell of sleeping. I pour another whiskey, pull the desk chair in front of the window, open both sashes along with the thick, wood-slat shutters. The noise, the cool air, and the sweet, smoky smells of the narrow, cobbled street below speak to me. They say, *You are far away from home, Dick Moonlight.*

I light a cigarette and whisper back at the voices. "I couldn't agree more," I say.

My voice sounds strange and dreamlike in the small room. It makes me feel self-conscious and aware of my existence, as though I were staring at my own beating heart through transparent skin and flesh.

I unfold the small piece of paper Francesco gave to me. I read the name of the man he wants me to see in the morning: Abdiesus. His stall is located on the corner of the Via Zannoni.

Abdiesus...not sure I can trust a man who has the word "die" in his name. But then I don't have much of a choice. I pocket the paper and sip more whiskey. I think about how strange my life has become in the past few days. How I've gone from a boring Sunday afternoon getting drunk in a corner bar while watching the New York Giants beat the Dallas Cowboys in the final minute of the fourth quarter, to spearheading an international mission to retrieve a flash drive that, should it fall into terrorist hands, could potentially spell death and destruction for a whole lot of people. Innocent people. Moonlight the courageous. Or maybe, Moonlight the perpetually in over his broken head.

Listen: I've found myself in surreal situations before. But this one tops them all. What I mean to say is, I'm Dick Moonlight, after all. Captain Head Case. Suicide survivor. A man who lives minute to minute due to a piece of .22 caliber hollow-point pressed up against his cerebral cortex. If I die right at this moment with a burning cigarette in my hand and a glass of Jack in the other, it would come as no surprise. So why then choose me for such an important mission?

I guess the answer lies somewhere in between love and expendability.

Lola and I love—used to love—one another as much as any tight sig others can. If I have to guess, I'd say that despite going off with Barter, she still loves me. And if she still loves me, then perhaps she will trust me enough to reveal the location of the flash drive. That is, if Barter and/or Clyne has revealed its location to her in the first place, which my built-in shit detector tells me doesn't even fall into the ballpark of possibilities. Still, stranger things have happened.

But there's more to this than just the Moonlight/Lola Ross connection. If I were to suddenly buy the farm while going after the flash drive, the agencies involved could at least say they did everything in their power to get it back, including enlisting the very man who placed it into the wrong hands in the first place. If the mission were to fail, they might wash their hands of any and all responsibility in allowing me access to the flash drive in the first place. Because, in essence, that is where the FBI made their initial mistake. They never should have trusted me with it once it was discovered that Czech had hidden it under my personal table at Moonlight's Moonlit Manor. I wanted Clyne to have it. Not the FBI. I liked Clyne, felt sorry for him now that his wife walked out on him. I've got a soft spot for a man who's been cheated on and scorned by the woman he loved. At the time, I felt him a suitable caretaker of the flash drive. How was I to know he'd actually run away with it, put it up for sale on the black market?

Other factors might have been considered.

I'm a decorated vet of the first Iraq war. I know what it is to experience combat in a foreign land, know what it feels like to be shot at by people who want to kill you. People who don't speak your own language. I know how to use firearms with the intent to kill. I know how to use a fighting knife. I know all about the overriding importance of the quote, "mission," unquote. I know how to take orders.

And I know how to kill.

I know that before this mission is finished, it is likely that I will kill again. I also know that Crockett and her crew of agents know that my love for Lola overrides everything. Even my own life. No doubt, that is what they are betting on. And in the end, if I fail, they can use me as the patsy. They can put me in prison for having handed off the flash drive to Clyne in the first place and for having written that "terroristic" letter to the IRS.

So perhaps it makes perfect sense that I'm sitting in front of an open window, staring out onto the Florentine night with a left hand throbbing from a knife attack that nearly cost me my pinky finger.

What a beautiful, cool night it is. Clear, with the second full moon this month casting its glow down upon my face.

Blue moonlight.

CHAPTER 26

I'm up early the next morning, my head a little crusty from the Jack on top of, at best, one hour of restless sleep, my good hand gripping the automatic.

My pinky finger still throbs, but at least my bruised balls are back in action.

After last night's attack, I'm leaving nothing to chance. Before I get dressed I take a few minutes to maneuver the bones and joints in my injured hand. Despite the stitches and the bone-deep gash it suffered, there's no real swelling to speak of. It's throbbing and sore, but I can use the hand in a pinch. I just thank God it's not my shooting hand.

As I pop a couple of Advil with some no-gas aqua mineral, I wonder if the Russian really intended to cut my finger off. Or was he only pretending to do so? Either way, it was one hell of a painful experience and one that I won't soon forget.

That Russian goon and I...we'll meet again. When we do, I won't make the same mistake he did. I'll not only cut off one of his fingers for real, but I'll cut off his trigger finger. One more Russian mobster out of business won't hurt my chances of survival. Not by a long shot.

* * *

I shower, holding my injured hand outside the curtain. After I dry off, I put my black pants back on, along with the combat boots, lacing them all the way to the top. They're snug and fit like a second skin. If I need to sprint myself out of a situation, I can count on them like I can my favorite pair of running shoes. Cutting off more duct tape from the roll Francesco loaned me, I tape the .22 to the top of the left lace-up boot.

Then, slipping on a thin black turtleneck over a long-sleeved T-shirt, I drape the elastic shoulder holster over my head. I retrieve the .9 mm from between mattress and the bed board, thumb back the clip release, allow the magazine to drop into the palm of my hand, just short of coming all the way out of the pistol grip. All the rounds are there like I knew they would be. Slapping the clip back home, I slide back the bolt and open the chamber. I deposit an extra round into the barrel and gently release the chamber closed, thumbing on the safety.

An extra round in the chamber wouldn't hurt my odds of survival either.

The piece secure in the holster, grip-first for easy access, I then slide a fighting knife and its leather sheath onto my belt. Buckling the belt, I grab my leather coat and put it on. With two additional ammo clips stuffed into the interior pockets and my sunglasses masking my eyes, I'm ready to make my way out the door to the busy marketplace where I'm supposed to find an Iranian by the name of Abdiesus.

I have a decent idea of where I'll find his leather-goods stall, but still I feel like I might be looking for a sewing needle in a stack of sewing needles.

But then my gut speaks up and tells me that I don't have to worry about recognizing Abdiesus.

In all probability, he will already know me.

CHAPTER 27

Here's what I learned in college, just before coming to Florence for the first time as a young man: leather has been big business here since the Romans founded the place more than two thousand years ago when, for some reason that defies all conventional logic, they decided to place a soldiers' encampment on the swampy, mosquito-infested valley. To further defy logic and wisdom, the area became a stopping-off point for travelers and adventure seekers of all kinds. Merchants seeking trade who originated from all ends of the known earth. Spice merchants from India. Chinese selling textiles. Persians selling rugs, bronze cookware, swords, knives, animals, and even slaves who would become gladiators.

The markets have remained for all these years, making the city a vibrant melting pot of hawkers, bargain hunters, and adventurers. And the police rarely make an appearance inside its tidal river of people.

It's been awhile since I've traipsed through the tent-covered markets. But here's what I know: it's easy to get lost inside them and even easier to get pulled away and abducted.

Especially when you're traveling alone to a place where you have enemies. Mortal enemies.

* * *

I head down the flights of stairs to the Via Faenza. I hook a right and head toward the busy four corners where Faenza crosses over Nazionale. On the opposite left-hand corner stands a policeman, his blue uniform tight over a hard body, black-shaded sunglasses hiding eyes that just might be staring me down. Sharing the corner with him is a beggar with bare, hobbled feet that resemble dark, scaly, distorted tree branches. Carlo comes to mind. The half man, half beast, with hooves for hands and feet. I think about our immediate moment of connection. My own sliced hoof throbs in my pocket.

Behind the cop and the beggar is a newsstand that sells newspapers, drinks, lottery tickets, and souvenirs that include underwear mimicking Michelangelo's *David*. Not the whole *David*, but his infamous *package*.

There's also a large poster mounted to the exterior wall outside the store in a glass frame. The poster depicts the levels of Dante's hell, or Inferno. Peering over my left shoulder, I cross Nazionale as soon as the traffic permits. My eyes still glued to the Inferno poster, I don't have the time to study all the levels since I'm simply passing by while trying not to raise the attention of the cop. But I look at it long enough to make out a level entitled "Gluttony." The word appears over an illustrated landscape of darkness, hard rock, filthy mud, filthy water, and a heavy cold rain.

Another level bears the headline "Wrath." People trying to stay afloat in a fast-moving river while they lash out at one another.

In another level, called "The Violent," naked bodies are burning while dogs with humanlike faces stab at them with pitchforks. It's not hard to recognize the face of Hitler in this level. Also, I clearly see Napoleon, Oppenheimer, and Osama bin Laden. The perfect poster for your teenage kid's bedroom.

Now that I'm past the newsstand I pick up my pace along the narrow, cobble-covered street. Past cheap trattorias and sandwich shops, past shops run by Asians selling only cheap beer and wine, past sexy-underwear stores, and one store that sells custom-made masks, some of which look Satan-inspired, with their grossly long noses and evil, bulging eyes. The road is filled with Americans, Peruvians, Germans, Africans, Iranians, Syrians, you name it.

There are *Italians in Italy, right?*

I walk past tourists and art students, both young and old, and I feel the good weight of the .9 mm tucked away in the shoulder holster bobbing gently against my rib cage. If I could wear it on my right hip I'd feel like Clint Eastwood in a spaghetti Western.

The Good, the Bad, and the Head Case...

I go left at Via Zannoni and eye the first tent on the corner to my right. There are two steady streams of leather-hungry tourists congesting the narrow path between the two long parallel rows of tents and booths, but that shit doesn't concern me. When I spot the little waif of a man seated behind the tent, my gut tells me I'm looking at Abdiesus.

I approach the man carefully, so as not to startle him. He's so little and suntanned dark I feel like a sudden start might cause him to crack down the middle.

I'll say it again: he's a little man. Skinny. Dark-skinned, dressed in a gray or off-white thawb, an honest-to-goodness fez balanced on the back of his bald skull. He's old, maybe eighty or more, and sports a sparse white beard. The type of Middle

Eastern man who might get pulled out of line at airport security for a full anal cavity and shoe check back in the States. He's smoking a cigarette lovingly, like it's what he has now in the place of true affection, and it isn't until he's finished smoking it that he looks up at me.

I reach into my pocket, pull out the pack of Marlboros, thumb open the lid, silently offer him one. He reaches out with a hand that's as bone thin and brown leathery as the leather jackets and belts he sells on the other side of the tent. With long, bone-colored fingernails, he plucks out four cigarettes, sliding one into his mouth and the others into the chest pocket on his robe-like thawb.

I pull out the Bic lighter, fire it up for him.

"How much for one of your leather belts?" I pose. "I'm particularly interested in a black one."

He nods, smokes, stares at the burning end of the lit cigarette. Then, reaching out with his stick-thin right hand, he pulls one of the black belts from off the rack.

He stares at my waist.

"I will have to punch one or two new holes in the leather for your narrow waist."

Popping the cigarette between dry, cracked lips, he picks up a metal hole punch and, in a surprising display of strength, punches two new holes out of the leather belt. Coiling the belt and its metal buckle into a round, compact package, he slips it inside a brown paper bag, hands it to me. I slip the belt into my side coat pocket and dig out a twenty-euro note to complete the sale.

"Keep the change," I offer.

He writes up a receipt, hands it to me. I stuff it into my right pants pocket.

"You know who I am," I say after a beat. It's a question.

"I've never been to America," he says in a voice that's gravelly, soft, and sad. The voice of a man who has lost something precious to him, like a wife or a child or both. "Is it like they tell me it is?" he goes on while slowly, painfully sitting back down. "Corrupt and evil?"

I shake my head, light up a smoke of my own. "My country has its faults," I say, releasing a cloud of blue smoke that combines with his. "But it has a wonderful heart. And we care about people. Not just our own. I make no apologies for her."

"Is that why you have come for the flash drive, Mr. Moonlight?"

His question takes me by surprise. But I'm not sure why it should. It makes sense that he would know of my mission. Especially if Francesco filled him in on it. Naturally I'm concerned about trust. But it's a little late to be concerned about that now.

I smoke a little more. Then, "Yes. It's why I have come."

He crosses stick legs, revealing bony feet protected with leather sandals, and considers my answer for a moment. Just a few feet beyond us, the crowd moves at a steady, browsing pace. Rarely does someone stop to view Abdiesus's goods. Makes me wonder how he makes a living. But then something dawns on me.

I reach into my pocket, shave off two fifty-euro notes, go to hand them to him. He holds up his free hand. "Not now," he says. "There will be time for that after we have spoken."

I can't help but notice the plain gold band wrapped around his wedding finger.

"I understand," I say. "Buyers. Are there buyers like we've been hearing? Are you prepared to tell me who they are?"

"How will you utilize this knowledge, Mr. Moonlight?"

"The flash drive contains dangerous information that could be used against my country and other free countries should it fall into the wrong hands. Last time I heard, many Iranians weren't too fond of Americans."

He cocks his head. "I don't have a particular problem with Americans, Mr. Moonlight," he offers. "They might be loud and fat, but they spend money on my leather jackets. So how can I complain?"

"Your president isn't such a fan of our free market society. He also denies the Holocaust ever happened."

"Ahmadinejad is a cruel joke. A Nazi. A puppet of Supreme Islamic statehood. He is the Goebbels of my country. His words are air. Nothing more."

"Is he the one buying the flash drive?"

He laughs as smoke billows from his nostrils and mouth. "I like you, Mr. Moonlight. You think big."

"Is he?"

"It's possible the men who want the flash drive and are willing to pay one hundred million dollars for it are working for him. Yes, indeed, it is possible."

I take that as a definite yes.

He smokes the cigarette all the way down to the filter, then drops it to the street, where it rolls into the narrow linear space between the square-shaped cobbles. I half expect him to light up another, but he decides to give his lungs a rest for the moment.

"Listen carefully," he says. "The men you seek have been observing Mr. Clyne and Mr. Barter for days now. They have decided to reveal themselves in order to make the deal for the flash drive."

I feel a start in my heart. "When will this meeting you speak of take place?"

"In two days, inside the Palazzo Vecchio. At midday when the square is at its most crowded. Do you understand?"

I understand perfectly well. It means I have at most forty-eight hours to retrieve the flash drive or this thing is shot.

"Who are these men? What are their names?"

"None of those things are important, Mr. Moonlight," he says. "What's important is that you know they are serious investors and that they are most likely watching us right now." Lighting up one of the three Marlboros he has left. "Now that you have the knowledge you came for, you can pay me what you wish. Then you must go."

I hand him the two fifty-euro bills.

He looks up at me, the new cigarette burning between his lips. His deep steel-blue eyes scream *"More."*

I reach back into my pocket, pull out another fifty and two twenties. Hand them to him. He smiles, nods in thanks. "And..." he adds, gesturing toward the chest pocket where I store the box of Marlboros. I get the hint. I hand them over.

He smiles.

"May I ask you a question?" I pose.

He nods.

"Why are you willing to hand over this information when it must place you in considerable danger?"

"How old would you say I am, Mr. Moonlight?"

"I don't know."

"Please be so bold as to venture a guess."

I stare into his leathery face. Into steel-blue eyes surrounded by mud-stained whites streaked with jagged broken vessels of blood red.

"Eighty," I guess. "Eight-five."

He laughs again. "I will celebrate my sixty-third spring in March of next year," he informs.

I feel a shot of ice-cold liquid shoot up and down my backbone. I feel the eyes of the Iranian buyers lasering into my skin and flesh. I eye the many tourists coming and going, listen to their nonstop banter coming at me in an endless variety of languages.

"I was once a rich man," he goes on. "I went to college and owned a leather factory in Tehran. I had a wife and three sons. This is back in the good days before the Islamist revolution and the shah was overthrown."

"The shah lived rich at the expense of his people," I say. "That's what I've been taught."

"The shah provided my country with a stable economy and the freedom to earn much money. When he was deposed, my sons joined the revolution. Today they are dead, hanged by their own people for insubordination when the day came to steal my factory, my money, my possessions, and my house in the name of Allah and the revolution."

I swallow something hard and bitter. "And your wife?"

"Raped before my eyes and beheaded. When the student radicals were done, they tossed her severed head into my lap and laughed at me. A week later I agreed to speak with your CIA about my experiences and to become an extra pair of eyes and ears for them. Twenty years ago they smuggled me out and brought me here. I have never been back to Iran since that time."

Looking into this man's eyes, I can see that the pain of his loss is still fresh. The death of his family did not occur a generation ago, but only moments ago.

VINCENT ZANDRI

"Thank you," I whisper just as a middle-aged American man wearing a fanny pack approaches the tent. Abdiesus stands, faces the chubby American.

"You wish to purchase a leather jacket?" he asks.

"You ain't gonna try and rip me off, are you, Abdul?" barks the American.

"I give you good price," Abdiesus says. "I wish for you only happiness."

Our eyes meet for one more brief second, and the depth of his suffering flashes inside his. I turn and leave as the American tries to fit himself into a brown leather jacket that can't possibly be zipped over his beer gut.

CHAPTER 28

I head back across Zannoni to Faenza.

I'm not three steps into my stride before I feel them in back of me. Two men following me from a distance of about twenty feet. I catch their transparent reflection in a plate-glass window when I stop and pretend to stare into a storefront filled with expensive sweets. The tall, football-player-sized one from last night and a short one who might have also been a part of the threesome who nearly cost me a fingertip. Russian goons, just like the Obamas from the night before. But instead of Obama masks they're wearing sunglasses. I'm not sure they'd fit in here with Obama masks covering their mugs.

I start walking again, and they start following.

They must have been tailing me when I met up with Abdiesus. If they think I know the location of the flash drive, they will follow me until I lead them to it, and then they will kill me and dump my body into the Arno. Or maybe they have somehow gotten wind of the upcoming meet between the three amigos and the Iranian buyers. I feel a cold wave flash up and down my backbone. My throat constricts and the soreness returns to my gut, like I've once more been kicked in the groin. If the Russians are aware of the meeting, they'll no longer feel the need to keep me alive. They'll kill me. They'll torture me for fun and kill me and toss my sad carcass in the river.

They follow, not even pretending to hide themselves, or their faces. Why bother with the Obama masks anymore? They were willing to torture me in order to get what they wanted. My throbbing pinky finger is evidence of that. My premature death nearly a year ago from a senseless beating in an Albany back alley is evidence of that. The surgical staple they plucked out of my side with a bowie knife is evidence of that. And now that it's likely they know all about the meeting with the Iranians, they will cut to the chase and eliminate me once and for all.

Me walking and the Russian goons following.

We could go on like this all day.

What to do...

I run.

CHAPTER 29

I jerk a right down a narrow alley and out into the Piazza Santa Maria Novella. Behind me, I hear them screaming at one another in Russian. I hear leather soles slapping against cobblestones. I hear my heart pounding in my temples. Looking back, I see them coming. The goons sprinting after me, automatics drawn.

It's gonna be a shootout in Florence. The Wild West meets the Renaissance.

I reach inside my coat, pull out my piece, thumb back the hammer.

I stop, turn, plant a bead on the big one.

They split up and nosedive to the pavement just as I squeeze the trigger. Twice.

The rounds ricochet against the old cathedral, taking a group of Japanese tourists by surprise. They scream.

I aim lower, squeeze off another round. The sidewalk at the big one's head explodes, sending shards of concrete and stone into his face. The Walther is definitely a short-range pistol. It's hard planting a bead at this distance, but not impossible.

I get one off at the smaller one.

Same thing: concrete explodes in his face, followed by shrieks and screams from the Japanese sightseers.

Then, from out of the shadows cast by the tall church just to the side of them, a four-legged animal appears. Only this four-legged animal isn't a wild animal. It's a man.

It's Carlo, the man/dog.

He's growling and biting at the big Russian's pant leg. He's viciously going at the leg, tearing off clothing and skin. The terrified Russian yanks his leg away from the man/dog's rabid mouth, crabs backward until free. When he manages to get to his feet, he and the short Russian sprint their way out of the plaza in the opposite direction of Carlo and me.

Sirens.

The police are coming.

Carlo canters his way over to me, all grins. "You like my performance, New York?" he poses.

"I'm in trouble."

"Head for the markets," he insists. "Disappear in there. No one will find you. Go now."

A former marine, I know to follow orders without hesitation. Even if they're coming from a man who walks like a dog.

I make a mad dash for the markets, back the way I came across the Via Faenza to the Via Zannoni to the congested marketplace.

I spot Abdiesus as I make my way past his tent. He looks at me, smiles.

I know precisely what he's thinking.

Just another day for Dick Moonlight, Captain Head Case.

CHAPTER 30

I head back to the Il Ghiro safe house, or should I say *un-safe* house, bound up the stairs two at a time, head directly to my room without looking to see if Francesco is occupying his office. It's only when I close the door behind me that I notice how hard my heart is beating and my injured hand is throbbing. And holy crap, have I got to pee or what?

Engaging the deadbolt on the door, I head into the bathroom.

I pull myself out, begin to relieve myself. If you've ever felt like you're standing inside a fishbowl, then you know the feeling: like someone is not only standing behind you, but two more invisible people are standing on either side of you. Even though you're four-walled, the sensation of eyes glaring at you is enough to make your knees tremble. If you're trying to pee at the time, you can pretty much forget about it until you make a check on your perimeter.

I zip up, pull my automatic.

To the left of the toilet is a sink and above that a mirror. The bathroom is small, so the mirror reflects the scene behind me in full Panavision. I want to look into the mirror, but at the same time, I dread what I'm about to see. I do it anyway.

The plastic shower curtain is snow white and semitranslucent. Through the curtain I make out the figure of a man. It sends my heart shooting up into my throat.

I whip my body and the automatic around.

"It's face time, asshole!"

The figure behind the curtain doesn't move.

Trigger finger at the ready, I reach out with a trembling hand, tear the curtain off the metal rings. The curtain falls, revealing the truth. There's a man behind the curtain.

A dead man.

CHAPTER 31

My Italian contact hangs from a cast-iron ceiling pipe by the neck. His own fine Tuscan leather belt serves as his noose. Eyes wide open, his blue tongue sticking out at me like he's only pretending to be a dead guy who's been hanged in a shower stall. But I know he's not pretending to be dead, because dripping into the shower basin is the blood that emerges from the gash in his neck, which is located just below the leather belt.

In my head I see the masked man with the bowie knife gripped in his hand. I see him using it on my new friend's neck.

I hope for Francesco's sake it was a quick death.

It dawns on me then that I might not be alone inside that guest room. The possibility of an enemy presence lodges itself in my throat and in my gut like a Russian hammer and sickle.

I step out of the bathroom, turn ever so slightly to my right, and eye the closet door, then the rest of the room. There's nothing else inside the safe house but dead Francesco and the closet's contents, which include the possibility of people who want to kill me.

Want. To. Kill. Me.

I plant a bead on the closet and empty all nine rounds into it.

* * *

When the smoke clears, I release the clip and slap home a fresh one. Even though the wooden door is a splintered relic of what it had once been, I approach with extreme caution, prejudice, and paranoia.

I throw open what's left of the closet door closest to me, and it simply disintegrates in my hand.

The good news is the closet is empty.

The bad news is the rush I begin to feel of adrenaline-laced arterial blood to my overstressed and bullet-damaged brain.

The even badder news is that I pass out on the spot.

CHAPTER 32

There are people who will tell you that it's impossible to dream when you pass out. Bullshit. These are the same dolts who will tell you nobody dreams in color. Again, bullshit.

I do both.

Just like I am now...

In the dream I'm running down a narrow back alley of Florence. There are three men chasing me. They have guns in their hands. Automatics. They're wearing Obama masks. They are dressed in black. They are yelling at me in Russian, so I don't understand a word they're saying.

When they start shooting at me, I feel the bullets enter into my back. I feel the hard kick and the sting of the hot steel entering my flesh. I fall forward, I'm about to hit the solid rock cobbles head-on—but find myself falling through them. Falling right through stone, down into a black space until I come to a dark place surrounded by water...

I'm all alone, sitting on this mud-covered rock, staring out into a vast nothing. Just cold ocean. But soon people start to gather. Like me they are all alone, but unlike me they all seem to be oblivious to one another. They just look lonely and forlorn, like they've been banished from somewhere, like heaven maybe. A great wind blows across the rock and seeps into our bones. Behind me, one of the dead, this one a woman, wails in lonely agony and begins digging in the mud. Suddenly aware of my dead presence, she starts tossing great chunks of mud at me...

And then I fall some more.

This time I land in a river. There are other people floating in the river. I'm having trouble keeping my head above water. I'm swallowing rancid-tasting water and sinking. But soon I come to a riverbank and someone or something pulls me out and lays me out onto the mud-covered shore along with a whole bunch of other moaning dead people. The sky is murky and thick, but it's daytime. Flashes of lightning strike all around me and explode in thunderous quakes.

From out of nowhere a series of massive stone wheels start rolling toward us, crushing the people along the way. Each one of the stone wheels is as big as a house, and they are headed right for me. I want to move out of the way but I can't. I'm paralyzed and helpless. From behind me I hear a laugh. Evil, squealing laughter. When the first stone begins to roll over my feet, I feel the bones, skin, and flesh being crushed...

And then I fall some more.

When the fall stops I find myself naked and on fire. There's a monster standing over me. It's a half-man, half-beast kind of thing with one eye in the center of its forehead. It's holding a pitchfork and it's prodding me with it, drawing blood each time. The stabs are agonizing, but the wounds heal themselves as fast as they are inflicted. The fire burns and tortures, but the skin remains whole and undamaged, as do my nerves. The people around me are all men, and similar beasts are torturing them. I recognize some of the men. There's Napoleon and Hitler to my right. To my left, J. Robert Oppenheimer and Lee Harvey Oswald are sharing an anguished laugh. Not far behind them, the Islamic extremists who took down the Twin Towers with two fully fueled 747s.

How the hell did I end up here?

In hell.

I'm not evil.

I don't kill people.

Well, scratch that. I do kill people. I mean, I have killed people. But they were the evil ones. I didn't want to have to kill them. It just happened.

I look up at the beast, into its one-eyed face.

He stabs me yet again with the pitchfork, making my chest feel like it's being ripped open. This time, instead of pulling the pitchfork back out, the beast leaves it in there...

When I come to, I feel a dull pain in the center of my chest.

I roll over, land on top of my mobile phone. My hand is trembling when I thumb the speed dial for my FBI contact, Agent Crockett. As the phone rings, I try to calculate what time it is on the East Coast of the US. It's about five in the morning. I'm going to be waking her up. But then, I'm sure the brutal murder of my Italian contact is a pretty good excuse.

The phone connects.

"Agent Crockett's phone," I hear in a man's deep, dry voice.

Agent Zumbo. Tell me it ain't so...Crockett and Zump together. I picture his naked barrel stomach rubbing up against her tight little body. Shudder away the image as if it were spider crawling on my face.

"Zumbo, it's Moonlight. Where's Crockett?"

"Say it in Italian, sweetie," he answers with a belly laugh. Like this is all some kind of a joke.

"Fuck you, Zump!" I scream. "Get me Vanessa Crockett."

"She's a little indisposed at the moment. How can I be of assistance?"

More images of a naked Zump together with Crockett. I'm going to have to burn my brain when this is finished.

"It's fucking five in the morning. She's got to be still in bed."

"Not us, Moonlight. We're working. Pulling yet another all-nighter to make sure your mission succeeds...you know, the one you'd better pull off if you don't want to spend the rest of your life getting fucked up the ass by some black bull stud in a four-by-seven prison cell."

I'm not sure why I feel relieved the ex-football star doesn't appear to be presently bedding down with the female agent, but I can't help but feel that way. Then comes a commotion, another Zump belly laugh. I'm guessing the phone's been snatched from his hand.

"Mr. Moonlight," comes the female voice. "I asked you not to call unless it's an absolute emergency." It's Crockett.

"Tell you what, Agent Crockett," I say, lifting myself from the floor and heading back into the bathroom. "I got something I want you to see." I snap a picture of Francesco and forward it as a multimedia text. "Take a look at that and tell me if what you see does not, in fact, constitute a fucking emergency."

While the image transmits it dawns on me that I have yet to take the piss I so badly needed to take ages ago. Holding the phone between my right cheek and shoulder, I unzip, pull myself out, and wait for some sign that Crockett received the picture. It comes in the form of an exhale.

"OK, Moonlight," she says. "Here's what I'd like you to do: gather your things and leave that place."

"What about the body?"

"Leave it. We have people who will take care of it. You're in danger there, obviously enough. Security has clearly been breached and your cover is entirely blown. Whoever did this to your contact will do the same to you if they find you there. Leave."

"You don't have to tell me twice. Any ideas where I might find a safe roof over my head until I can find the flash drive?"

"I don't think that will be possible. Abort the mission and come home."

"Not a chance. I came here to collect the flash drive and to save all humanity. That's what I'm going to do."

"Bravo for you, Moonlight, although the truth is that you went to Florence to save your girlfriend."

"She's a part of the package."

"I'll try to find you a place to hide out. In the meantime, keep a low profile until you hear from me."

"When will that be? There's these Russian bastards who know precisely where I'm—"

Call ended. Crockett has hung up on me before I can even finish my sentence. My ass is on the line and she cuts off communication.

No time for brooding.

Time instead for peeing.

When I'm done, I fill up my pack with all my things, strap it over my shoulder. I pack up the computer. Unlocking the deadbolt, I slowly make my way out into the narrow hall, my .9 mm leading the way. When I come to the guesthouse door, I slowly open it and slip on out, careful to make sure no one is waiting for me on the landing. Then I haul ass down six flights of stairs and out into the streets of Florence, a most beautiful and unhealthy place.

CHAPTER 33

I make a check of my watch face.

Noon.

I'm trying to think of a place I can go without risking being spotted by a whole bunch of Russian goons who want to see me dead. Then it dawns on me. The Uffizi Palace art gallery. It will be packed with students, tourists, art experts, artists, and some of the most crack Italian police and security guards in the country. It's just a matter of getting my automatic past that same security.

In terms of weaponry, I'm a walking arsenal. I'm carrying the .9 mm in a shoulder holster along with two of the three original additional nine-round clips. I've got a fighting knife strapped to my belt and another .22 snub-nose five-shot revolver duct taped to my lower left leg. I'll be more or less protected in the Uffizi, but no way I'm heading in there unarmed. If the Russians follow me into that place, they will somehow manage to do so along with their own personal hand cannons.

But that doesn't mean I can walk in with every lethal tool I'd like to have on hand to defend myself against former Russian soldiers turned mobsters.

Within sight of the Uffizi, I spot a Dumpster inside a narrow alley positioned perpendicular to the Piazza della Signora.

Actually, a series of three small plastic and metal Dumpster on wheels that collect both refuse and recyclables. Thank God for a green Italy.

I sneak a quick look over both shoulders, make an about-face to see what's happening behind me. All clear, I head to the Dumpster and kneel down before the one in the center. I rip the tape from my boot and release the .22. Then I unsheathe the fighting knife and pull out the two remaining .9 mm clips.

Down on my knees, I feel around underneath the Dumpster, searching for a place that will effectively conceal the weaponry while also allowing me easy access should I return to this place on the run. I locate just such a space beside the left front wheel: a flat piece of metal attached to the mobile Dumpster's chassis. I slip the stuff onto it, careful to set the pistol grip and knife handle so that they face me.

Standing, I take another look around, heft my pack up onto my back, and head back up the road, until I come to the square. From there I turn left and make the short trek to the Uffizi Palace, a museum guarded by an eight-foot-tall Perseus. The Greek god holds a sword in one hand and the decapitated head of Medusa in the other.

CHAPTER 34

The Uffizi is a long, concrete-and-stone structure that wraps around a rectangular courtyard. All the floors aboveground are supported by thick pillars. Displayed in between the pillars are statues of all the great Renaissance geniuses, like Brunelleschi, who designed the Duomo, and my friend Dante Alighieri, the writer who lately has been plaguing my dreams with his particular version of hell.

My. Hell.

Moonlight the doomed and the damned.

I enter into the No. 2 entrance, where the ticket window is, and purchase a day pass for fifteen euros. Then I head to the No. 1 entrance and the long queue that's already formed outside it. I take my place at the back. There's a Japanese girl in front of me. She's got colorful tattoos on her neck and the backs of her hands. I imagine the tattoos run up the length of her arms, but her worn leather biker jacket is concealing them. What it doesn't conceal is her tall, gravity-defying punk-rock Mohawk. It's painted bright red. Around her neck, a chain-link dog collar. Timeless punker fashion. Standing directly before her is an old woman, and in front of her, an entire group of Japanese tourists of all ages. Doesn't take me long to figure out they're all a part of the same tour group.

I feel the weight of the automatic hanging on my shoulder, and I know that I have to figure out a way to smuggle it in with me. Over my shoulder, I watch the people coming and going inside the open square. Some are sitting for the painters who have set up easels at various positions throughout the cobbled square. In between them, uniformed police casually walk from one end of the square to the other, their sunglass-shielded eyes peeled for security breaches, big or small. Wasn't that long ago a terrorist cell exploded an IED here, killing half a dozen innocent bystanders and wounding another two dozen.

The line moves.

The Japanese are granted access, two by two, by a pair of armed guards manning the entrance. The tourists are giddy, happy and excited, their beaming, ear-to-ear smiles reflected in the safety-glass doors as they enter into the building and approach security.

When it's time for me to enter, I'm not smiling. I'm walking a fine line, hiding my face in a way that enables me to avoid making eye contact with the two burly guards without *seeming* to be hiding it. I don't want them to see the stress and strain that must surely paint my face. I walk the line, I guess, because I'm allowed inside.

So far so good.

Then I see the airport-like security operation they have going here. A full-body scanner and baggage X-ray machine.

So far *not* so good.

I tell myself to think quick or face almost certain police arrest.

That's when the not-so-nice idea comes to me.

CHAPTER 35

The Japanese tourists are packed together tightly, even though they don't require packing together tightly, far as I can see. Must be a cultural thing. Conditions couldn't be better suited for what I'm about to do.

Sticking out my booted left foot, I trip the punk rocker as she attempts to move forward.

She doesn't drop so much as she careens into the old woman in front of her. They both fall, their bags and the contents they contain scattering loudly all about the stone floor.

Chaos ensues, and the guard operating the body scanner starts shouting, "Stop! Stop!" in accented English.

The old lady is wailing something and at the same time trying to gather her things, which have dispersed even beyond the body scanner. That's when I go to work.

I drop my pack and computer case onto the belted baggage scanner, then move ahead in the line and drop to one knee, offering my help to the old lady. The punk rocker whom I tripped is also trying to help her. I dip down almost flat to the tile, as though reaching to gather the poor lady's things. As the old woman sniffles painful tears and the punk rocker tries to assist her, I slip my automatic from its holster and slide it under one of the two cloth bags that lie on the floor. Then I push it beyond the body scanner.

All apologies and bumbling, stumbling helpfulness, I stand and cut the line, stepping on through the body scanner. The buzzer-like alarm goes off. I smile and offer an apology to the guard, who by now is more annoyed with all the commotion than concerned about imminent danger. I also offer a heartfelt apology to the little Japanese man whom I cut in front of.

"So sorry," I say.

But he just issues me a smirk. Rude line cutting must also be standard operating procedure in Japan.

The guard uses his electronic paddle to give me a full up and down body scan. It doesn't register anything until it comes to my head.

"I have this condition," I tell the guard. "There's a piece of bullet lodged in my brain."

He looks at me like I possess two of the aforementioned heads instead of one. But he's so annoyed he just waves me on. I grab my pack and my computer bag, and then I quickly bend down and pretend I'm retrieving the old lady's bag for her when in fact I'm picking up my automatic and shoving it into my leather coat.

I hand her the bag.

I'm happy to see she's stopped crying and hasn't broken anything like a hand or a hip. I gaze into the young Japanese punker's eyes. Rather, she gazes into mine, with eyes rimmed by black mascara. She nods, her red-painted lips tight.

"Sorry," I mouth.

She makes like a toy pistol with her right hand and mouths, "Bang! Bang!"

Oh shit.

I make my way over to baggage check, praying to God the punk rocker isn't a tattletale.

CHAPTER 36

My pack and computer securely checked, I head up four long flights of worn marble steps, eyes in the back of my head. When I come to the top, I hand the ticket taker my ticket stub and enter into the narrow but ornate first corridor. The ceilings are painted with scenes from Renaissance Florence's history. Palaces and cathedrals under construction, residents dressed in the formal, colorful garb of the day, gathering in piazzas that still look the same six hundred years later. The tops of the walls are framed in gold leaf. Below that can be found the hundreds of portraits of dignitaries who have come and gone throughout the centuries. Adventurers from distant lands like China and Africa, military men, bankers, artists, writers, scientists, and, of course, the hooked-nosed faces of all the Medicis, the people who financed the Renaissance with cash, greed, and blood.

I walk, trying to blend in with the hordes of people coming and going from the galleries to my left. I enter into the first room, come upon a giant painting of a chubby Madonna holding an even chubbier baby Jesus. Next to it, a graphic depiction of an adult Jesus hanging from a wood cross, metal nails pounded through his palms and joined feet. What a lot of people don't know is that he could not have been crucified that way. The soft tissue of the palms would have torn and he would have dropped from the cross. The more likely scenario is that Christ was crucified through the bones of the wrists to support his entire body weight. He would then have died from exposure and slow asphyxiation. Displayed directly beside the crucifixion painting, the freshly decapitated head of John the Baptist set on a silver platter. The Bible sure is pleasant.

I feel the hard steel of a pistol barrel press up against my lower spine.

"Don't say any words, Mr. Moonlight. Or I shoot your balls off."

The voice is deep and guttural. English spoken with a harsh Russian accent. How the hell did he get a hand cannon past security so easily? Maybe the Russians have friends on the inside. Maybe Italian security can be bribed. Too bad I didn't think of that. Would have prevented a whole lot of pain and confusion for some innocent Japanese tourists, an old lady among them.

"Not a great place for a cold-blooded killing, is it, Boris?" I say, my eyes still staring at John the Baptist's head and the blood dripping down from the hacked-away flesh on the neck, drop by thick red drop.

"I've killed in worse place. More public place, *da*?"

I'm looking at the black-leather-jacketed goon's reflection in the painting's glass frame. It's definitely Boris. The one whose knee I shot off almost one year ago while he lay in the backseat of my best pal Georgie's vintage orange Volkswagen Beetle. Why did he choose to lose his knee? Because he chose not to reveal the whereabouts of Lola, when I asked him so politely. Through the glass I can see that he has trouble standing still, and that he leans desperately to his right side.

"Knee still giving you trouble, Boris?" I say.

"I have been fitted with new knee," he answers. "It is plastic kneecap."

"You can't kill me, Boris," I say. "For one, the guards in this place would be on you like flies on borscht. And for two, you need me to bring you to the fleshy box, remember?"

"You are out of job, yes?" he snarls. "We know fleshy drive will be handed to Iranian buyers perhaps tomorrow afternoon. You are no longer needed alive. You are now nothing but dead fowl."

"Dead duck, Boris," I say. "Dead. Fucking. Duck. Get your fucking idioms right. And ducks aren't fowl. They're aquatic birds. My boy, Harrison, loves ducks. His bedroom walls were covered with them. I know about ducks, asshole. Alive ones. Not dead ones."

My eyes still gazing into John the Baptist's steel-blue eyes. Eyes that peer out at me like I am the last thing he will ever see before death overtakes him. Little known fact about sudden decapitation: the head lives for about thirty seconds, or until the oxygen runs out. I get the feeling the artist was well aware of this detail. You can see it in the eyes.

The pistol barrel pressed against my spine reminds me I have to think quick. I do it.

"There isn't going to be an exchange or a drop, Boris," I lie. "I thought you knew that."

"No drop. How can that be? My sources never wrong, *da*?"

"I don't know anything about your sources, but they missed the fucking boat on this one. The Iranians are out because they can't come up with the cash our three amigos are greedily insisting upon." Me, exhaling, staring into the eyes of a two-thousand-year-old dead man. "But you know what, Boris? I know where the flash drive is. I. Know. Where. It. Is. In fact, I'm working on getting ahold of it."

"We will work together, then, *da*? You and me, Mr. Moonlight, we will make the peace, stop all the senseless *bang bang* shooting and work on this together. Like Apollo/Soyuz. Like glasnost. Like Reagan and Gorby."

I laugh. "Yeah, something like that, Boris. I'm sure you're suddenly more trustworthy than my long-departed mom. Maybe you tried to pry some unconditional trust out of my friend Francesco before you hung him up in the shower and sliced his neck?"

"My sincerest apologies. He give us much trouble. He had nuclear-sized gun pointed at us. Quite dangerous and lethal, *da*?"

"Bet you're not really sorry, Boris. Bet you're lying."

"An unavoidable casual of wear Mr. Moonlight. Even you have killed in the heat of battle. You are no stranger to taking life."

In John the Baptist's eyes I see my future. Inside the bottom level of hell.

"No. God. No. Boris. In America, there's casualties of war and then there's casual wear. See what I'm saying? Get the difference?"

A couple of people try to get by. I have no choice but to stand my ground while Boris has the barrel of a pistol jammed against my spine. But when I look closer, I can see that it's the punk-rock Japanese girl from downstairs. The one who saw me pocket my automatic while trying to hand the bag back to the old lady.

I smile at her.

She smiles back, mouthing the words, "Bang, bang."

"Bang, bang," I mouth while cocking my head at Boris behind me.

She looks at him and then at me again. "Bad man?" she whispers with furrowed brow.

I close my eyes, nod slowly, as if to say, *Yes. Molto. Bad. Man.*

That's when I lift my right foot up and come down hard onto the foot attached to Boris's bad leg. I immediately shift to the right and go down onto my side as the silenced round makes a hole in John the Baptist's head.

Alarms sound.

Boris tries to back step, but his gimp leg seems to be planted in place. Gives me just enough time to pull out my .9 mm, roll over, rear both legs back, thighs against chest, and kick him in the bad knee.

He lets out a scream and drops to the floor, firing another round in my direction. The round drills a hole in the wood floor not six inches from my head.

People scream.

I bound back up onto my feet and make for the exit. Shoot a glance back. Boris getting back onto his feet, hobbling after me.

For a brief moment I think I can make it out of there since Boris is simply too slow to keep up. But the second I make it out into the hall, I run into another black-jacketed goon who's working the rooms in pursuit of me. It's the tall, football-player-sized goon. He plants a bead on me with his automatic, takes a shot that ricochets off the wood doorjamb. People are scattering, going down on their bellies. Parents becoming human shields for their kids. Between the screaming and the blaring alarm, the big goon's pistol doesn't need a silencer.

I make a run for it through the people, in the direction of the second Uffizi corridor and the area designated as "Café." I know from a previous visit that the café is outdoors. I know that if I can make it out there, I can make it over the wall and down into the piazza.

If only I can somehow manage to stay alive.

CHAPTER 37

I'm plowing through the people, praying I don't run into a team of guards.

On my tail is the second goon. Boris not far behind him. How he can keep up with a fake knee I have no idea. Desire means a lot in these matters.

I have my automatic gripped in my shooting hand. But I nearly killed an old lady smuggling it in here. I might as well use it.

Making the corner for the café, I stop dead in my tracks, about-face, drop down to one knee, assume a shooter's stance, squeeze one off at the big goon. Big motherfucker makes a great target, even when he ducks away for cover. I see the slight spray from the round as it grazes his left collar.

But it doesn't slow him down.

He straightens up and keeps coming at me, like a deer during hunting season that doesn't know it's been hit.

I stand, proceed to the café.

The patrons seated on the interior of the white marble and plate-glass walled café are already down on the floor, hiding under the tables. The alarm is blaring inside the place. I head out the glass door onto the terrace. A collective exhale of panic ensues from the people who occupy the round, umbrella-covered tables. I barrel through tightly positioned tables, tipping a couple over along with the bone-white espresso cups and sandwich plates set upon them. I move toward the knee-wall to a soundtrack of screams, breaking plates and glasses, and more rounds exploding all around me, kicking up shards of tile against my lower legs.

The knee-wall isn't a knee-wall exactly.

More like a wall constructed of both concrete pillars and metal grating that I'm forced to climb if I want to get my body over it. This is the hard part. Climbing. It's when I present a lovely full-body target. Might as well have a red bull's-eye painted on my ass. Lucky for me the big goon behind me is changing out his clip. That leaves me with maybe two or three seconds to play with.

I set my right foot onto the grating and begin to climb.

It doesn't take much effort to get to the top. But the lead has started flying again, and the rounds are whizzing by my head. A quick look over my shoulder reveals both the collar-injured big goon and Boris shooting at me. I wonder if I'm like the big goon—hit without knowing it. It can take up to an hour for the pain of a bullet to register. Either that, or these goons are not Putin's grade-A primo shooters. I flip my left leg around and begin to climb down onto the overhang. From there it's a fifty-foot drop down past the loggia into the Piazza della Signoria. But not if I shimmy my way to the far side of the ledge.

Like a lizard on a windowpane, I begin to shimmy.

CHAPTER 38

I'm clear of the gunfire.

But on the other hand, I've become quite the spectacle for the tourists who swarm among their tour groups inside the piazza. Some of the people scream with terror while others cheer me on in about half a dozen languages. A few people clap. Some Italians shout out, "*Vi! Vi! Vi!*"

Go! Go! Go!

I inch my way along, knowing I have a short window of opportunity to get myself free and clear of the Russians. Somehow I know they're not about to be contained by the Uffizi guards or the police. Every electric-charged, instinct-filled synapse in my body tells me to run and keep running.

I'm picturing the weapons I hid under the Dumpster. I need to get to them and then I need to get the fuck lost. When I come to the edge of the ledge, I have no choice but to climb the pillar down into the loggia, the open, porch-like area below the Uffizi café that houses a couple dozen massive sculptures. There's no way I can make my way all the way down the pillar. The first few feet of it are just too wide for my outstretched arms. But if I can manage to set my foot onto the small portion of sculpted cherub relief that protrudes from the wall and from there shift myself down along the top of the pillar, it's possible I can manage to grab a foothold onto the bronze statue of Perseus.

I slide down, inch by inch, and at the same time, reach out with my right foot until it supports my weight on top of the cherub's head. Leaning into the wall, I ease myself down until I set my injured left hand onto the cherub while releasing my right leg. The pain shrieks from my cut finger, shoots up and down my arm. But I manage to hold on. What the hell choice do I have? Now releasing my left leg, I manage to leverage my full body weight by hanging off the cherub with both hands, like a rock climber hanging by a piece of exposed rock. The pain in my hand is intense enough to rob me of my breath, but I hold on long enough to cradle the pillar with my legs.

Sliding down a few feet, I reach out with my right leg until the tip of my right boot touches Perseus's sword. By now the crowd has gathered all around the loggia. Happy, shiny, smiling faces. Maybe they think this is Florence's idea of performance art.

I inch down some more, until I have both my legs wrapped around the sword. When I'm confident I have a secure enough hold by clenching my legs into a pretzel, as if the sword were the bar on a jungle gym, I release my hold on the pillar.

That's how I come to find myself hanging upside down, staring at two Russian goons dressed in black leather barreling their way through the tourists, pistols gripped tight in their hands.

CHAPTER 39

To the collective roar of a now-panicked crowd, I monkey my way down the cold, bronze Perseus. Past his curly haired head, down his six-pack abs, onto the severed head of Medusa, and then a short drop to the concrete landing.

I don't bother with taking steps.

I jump the wall, onto the cobbled piazza, and sprint for the back alley where my weapons are hidden.

If I had to guess, I have maybe twenty-five steps on one Russian goon hobbled by a bad knee and another with a grazed shoulder. I can only hope they haven't called for backup, which they most surely have.

The answer to my question appears for me immediately.

As I take the corner into the alley, I see two more goons coming my way. One of whom is the short one with the big bowie knife who cut my finger and Francesco's neck. Or so I gotta believe.

These guys aren't fucking around.

They carry AK-47s. I dive for the Dumpster just as I see the spit of fire coming from the barrels. As the shots spray all around me, pinging off the cobbles and the metal Dumpster chassis, I grab the .22 and empty the five-round cylinder in their general direction. Dropping the revolver, I slap a fresh clip into the .9 mm and discharge it at the two men, forcing one man to take cover inside a doorway, but dropping the short one when a round pierces his neck.

That's for Francesco. And that's for my finger.

Standing, I finger off three more rounds into the doorway where one of the goons is still hiding. I pocket the one clip I have left and the .22, and re-sheath the fighting knife. Then I run, full sprint, in the direction of the Duomo. Like that was the plan all along.

I enter the Piazza del Duomo at an all-out sprint, coming to a stumbling stop when I catch the attention of a police officer to my left, who no doubt has been alerted to the crisis at the Uffizi. Sirens permeate the stone and ancient cement of Florence. My heart is pounding inside my head, blood-filled flesh squeezing out the temples. That bullet fragment just better sit tight inside my gray matter. It's all I can ever hope for.

The policeman appears frozen in place, then snaps into action toward me. I enter into a sprint once more. What the hell choice do I have?

To my right, I see two more men wearing leather coats and dark sunglasses. Their automatics might be concealed for now, but I recognize Boris and his injured lead goon plain enough. They're coming at me at a jogger's pace since that's the speediest pace they can manage, given Boris's bad leg and his lead goon's shot collar. Even so, they're closing the gap between me, the cop, and the massive white-and-green marble cathedral. A major part of me just wants to raise my weapon, plant a bead on them both, and make them instantly dead. But that would make me a cold-blooded killer in the eyes of the police. Maybe even the eyes of God. In my head I see the final level of Dante's hell. The final resting place for the violent and the murderous. Eternal damnation in the form of pitchforks, fire, and brimstone.

I have to make some kind of decision here. Make one quick.

Directly in front of me, there's a giant stone statue of Brunelleschi. The big, gray stone statue depicts the architect holding a compass in one hand and the other holding an open book. He's staring straight up at the top of the Duomo he built six hundred years ago, to the entire known world's amazement. But even from down on the ground, he seems to be looking into my eyes.

I look to my left: the Russian goons.

To my right: the cop pulling out his service automatic with his shooting hand while using his free hand to call for backup on his walkie-talkie.

I once more peer into Brunelleschi's gray eyes.

His stone mouth doesn't move, but his words speak to me clear as water.

I turn and make a mad dash for the Duomo.

The cop shouts at me to stop.

The Russians, as though oblivious to him, pull out their automatics and begin firing at will. The tour groups that queue all around the dome-topped cathedral duck for cover. I plow through them and enter into the side entrance, up the short flight of stairs, barrel my way past the ticket window before jumping the turnstile on my way to the interior staircase that leads to the holy Duomo interior.

God forgive me.

CHAPTER 40

The ancient staircase before me is narrow, made of stone blocks that have been stacked with a surgeon's precision. I start on the worn stairs, bounding them two at a time. The stairs corkscrew the circular rim of the dome precisely and seem never ending. Climbing them at a walk would be enough to make your heart beat in your throat. It's like running up a man-made mountain.

By the time I reach the first level, which empties out onto a narrow stone ledge that rims the dome's interior, I'm sucking serious wind. Displayed before me, like I've somehow died and entered into Judgment Day, are brilliant mosaics of men and women suffering at the hands of a horned devil right next to much luckier dead people who are languishing in the Lord's loving glow. I'm sweating bullets, panting my lungs out, and witnessing the culmination of good and evil, heaven and earth, the saved souls and the banished, blackened, tormented souls. But it's my mortal ass I'm more worried about saving at the present time.

As I'm coming out of the first stairwell I make out the strained voices of Boris and the injured goon. I know I can simply stand my ground at this point and just shoot the bastards as they emerge from the stairwell, but no doubt they've already figured that one out. They'll be ready for me. I glance down through a narrow window opening like the kind you'd find inside a medieval castle. Peer directly at Brunelleschi. He looks up at me, tells me to keep climbing.

The cathedral and its dome were built to allow man to diminish the impossible distance between heaven and earth. I enter into the second interior Duomo stairwell on my way to see God.

CHAPTER 41

My rotten luck...Dick Moonlight kind of luck.

Yet another Japanese tour group is on the way down.

The stairwell is simply too narrow for two full-grown human beings to pass without one of them pressing his or her back up against the stone wall. I don't bother with politeness. I pull out the .9 mm, shout out, "*Polizia!*"

It does the trick.

The Japanese group reacts as one, pressing their backs up against the circular wall, allowing me ample space to slip on through.

I continue my roundabout climb to the second level.

I bound through the stairwell door and onto another narrow stone walkway identical to the first one. Although this walkway also runs along the perimeter of the rotunda, it offers a much closer bird's-eye view of the Duomo's interior from just below the cupola. To my right, I once more come face to face with evil. I'm so close I feel like I can reach out and burn my fingers by touching the horned beast himself.

It's Dante's evil angel.

Satan.

The horned beast.

Gray-brown skin, black eyes, bald head, bat-like ears, and two bony horns topped off with sharp points. The keeper of the fire inside the lowest level of the inferno. He takes my breath away. I can only pray he is not my eternal future.

To my left I gaze out another narrow slit of a window, back down onto a piazza that's now far below. But I still see Brunelleschi looking up at me. Keep going, he tells me.

Vi! Vi! Vi!

I know better than to argue with a Renaissance genius.

Lungs flaming, I climb until entering into the third and final stairwell. I trek up the last flights of stone stairs until I reach the Duomo's top parapet walk. Pistol in hand, I ascend the short ladder that accesses the exterior. When my head emerges from the hatch-like opening at the top, I find myself surrounded by more Japanese tourists. A swarm of them occupy the parapet with their cameras and video cams.

Worked once: I climb all the way out and once more shout, "*Polizia!*" and then follow it up with "*Vi! Vi! Vi!*"

The tourists make a mad dash for the exit, leaving me alone at the top of the cultural world. Heading out onto the narrow exterior walk, I look for a way off the dome aside from simply jumping to my death. I make a quick inspection of the entire circular parapet.

The only way out of here is to climb down. This is not the most pleasant of prospects.

If I can get over the tower's metal suicide barrier and out onto the dome, it might be possible to slide down the tile ceiling and onto the cathedral roof. Possible. *Might* be.

Voices coming from the interior of the Duomo.

"Moonlight!" I hear. "Son of bitch! Moonlight mother-fucker! Dead man, Moonlight!"

I can either die here or take my chances out there.

I jump up, grab hold of the metal bars, and begin to chin myself up and over the suicide barrier, as if hell-bent on killing myself for real.

CHAPTER 42

I make it over the barrier as I hear at least one goon enter onto the parapet walkway. I cautiously ease myself down, ass-first, onto the copper flashing. The downward angle is sharp, but not so steep I can't keep my footing with my rubber-soled combat boots. Heart in throat, I take a crabwalking step out onto the orange/brown tiles. I feel the tile crunching and shifting under my feet. At this height, I feel the cool wind blowing against my face and against my sweat-soaked chest and neck.

Behind me, a limping Boris and his big goon are making their way around the narrow parapet walkway. I once more flash to the sliver of .22 caliber bullet in my head that, during times of extreme stress, can cause me to pass out. Now is not the time to pass out. Passing out would mean a fall of five hundred feet and certain death.

I continue my crabwalk out onto the dome, knowing that it will be impossible for Boris to follow me out here with his bad leg and just plain suicidal for a bigger-than-Zumbo-sized goon with a wounded collar to follow.

But then it's me…Dick Moonlight. Captain Head Case.

I've been known to be wrong on occasion.

A tile slides out from under me.

My right leg slips out and I drop down onto my ass, pressing my full body weight against the angled dome so that I don't begin a deadly slide over the side. More tiles come loose and skate off the dome. Coming from down below I hear the cries of the massive crowd that has gathered. I hear the sirens from the police cars and EMS vans. I know it's only a matter of minutes or seconds until helicopter rotors can be heard chopping through the cool air. What a television spot my presence on the dome will make.

Then I hear the crack of an automatic, and I know the Russians are shooting at me, as if they're shooting at the pigeons that nest up here. I want to look back at them but I can't. Both hands are pressed flat against the tile while the soles of my booted feet cling to the angled dome. Only a foot or two of rooftop separates me from a portion that's even more severely angled downward and will send me careening south like a helpless child falling down a schoolyard slide.

I look to my left and pick out the concrete seam that runs perpendicular to both the parapet and the base of the dome. I was so quick to get over the suicide barrier and onto the dome that I didn't think to look for some kind of support ladders roofing contractors must use during their constant repair work on the dome's tile roof. If the ladders exist, these concrete seams are all that could support them.

The wind picks up. It blows cold on my sweat-beaded face. My body begins to tremble while my injured left hand throbs up and down the length of the nerve bundles. But I hold on tight and run my eyes down the gray concrete seam.

It does indeed support a ladder. Rather, the metal rungs of a ladder are embedded into its concrete. Now it's just a matter of shifting myself the twenty feet to my left in order to access the metal rungs.

Sounds easy.

But not with a spray of bullets raining down on me from above.

CHAPTER 43

I don't give my next move any more thought.

I don't give the pain in my hand, the sweat burning my eyes, or the five-hundred-foot drop any more thought, either.

I just do it.

I begin to slide and crab my body to the left toward the concrete seam. That's when I see the injured goon to my right, crawling on his belly, a pistol in his hand aimed at me. He's wearing sunglasses, black pants, and a T-shirt. He's stripped himself of his leather coat, exposing the wound in his left collar. It's a larger wound than I thought. I didn't just graze him. I actually put one through him. Through the upper shoulder area. He must be supporting himself on his sheer size, strength, and loyalty to Boris, his boss.

He fires once and the round whizzes past. It's a near miss. But he's close enough that the second shot will likely find its target either in my head or chest.

No choice.

I pick myself up onto my feet and, leaning into the stiff wind and balancing myself like a man on a severely angled high-wire, make a run for the ladder.

I don't approach the ladder on foot so much as I dive for it.

I grab hold of the topmost rung with my good right hand and pray to God the rung holds without popping out of the old concrete.

I bear my entire weight upon it.

The rung pulls out from the concrete seam, sending my heart into my mouth. But it doesn't pull out the entire way. I have no choice but to find a foothold on a lower rung and begin the downward climb. It's exactly what I do.

I can only pray the concrete-embedded ladder rungs hold.

More bullets.

They zip past my head as the big Russian takes my cue and gets up on his feet. It's only a matter of time until one of those bullets connects. Problem is, the big goon has terrible aim. Maybe because he's got no sense of balance now that his shoulder has been shot through. He runs at me and shoots, all the time his body slowly sliding in toward the steep-angled dome. It's as if his feet are giving out from under him in slow motion. He doesn't make it another five feet before the black soles on his boots give way, as if the dome were alive and purposely slipping out from under him.

From where I'm holding on to the metal rungs, I see his dark eyes go wide, his mouth ajar with terror. The automatic slips out of his hand and careens down the dome, click-clacking its way over the tiles until it goes silently airborne, then cracks to the piazza. The goon tries to hold on by digging his fingernails into the tiles. An understandable but futile gesture because, let's face it, dude is truly fucked.

Gravity wins the day, and he begins to slide.

Slowly at first.

Then faster and faster, his chin bouncing over the tiles, fingernails scraping and tearing as he tries to stop his ever-speedier downward progress. He's eyeing me the entire time he's slipping, dropping, picking up speed. Until he's made it all the way down the length of the dome and disappears, falling as soundlessly as his weapon before joining it with a soggy thump on the cobbled piazza below.

CHAPTER 44

My entire body trembling, I descend what remains of the concrete-embedded metal rung ladder. Even from five hundred feet up on top of the tiled Duomo with the wind buffeting against my head, I'm hearing the horrified screams of the bystanders who gather around the dead Russian. For the first time all day I feel like I might live to see the sun set on sunny Italy.

I. Might. Live.

CHAPTER 45

I maintain a steady climb down, trying to look neither down nor up, but only at the concrete band just inches from my face. I descend as fast and as safely as I can until I come to the long, angled rooftop of the cathedral.

With the Russian goon having fallen to his death, much of the attention that had been focused on me must have shifted to his crushed remains. It's very possible the people are confusing him for me. He's the bigger man, but we are both dressed all in black, both wearing sunglasses, both carrying weapons. From a long enough distance or, in this case, height, the Russian fits my description to a T. If all those tourists are making this mistake, it's possible the police are too.

It takes only a few seconds for me to make it to the cathedral parapet. I climb up onto a narrow marble walkway that runs perpendicular to the cathedral roof and make a crouching search for a door or a trapdoor opening. I know there has to be some kind of access to the interior of the structure because it only makes sense that the rooftop be accessible for repairs.

I find what I'm looking for on the far side.

A small metal door with a skeleton-key padlock that's got to be almost as old as the cathedral itself. I press the barrel of the .9 mm against the lock and pull the trigger. The lock doesn't shatter so much as disintegrate.

Turning to face the small door, I search for a knob. Only there isn't one. Or there isn't one any longer. I raise up my right leg and kick in the ancient relic of a door.

A tight, narrow shaft appears for me. If I had to guess, I would say the shaft hasn't borne witness to a human presence in centuries. I enter into it anyway, patting my pants pocket for my Bic lighter.

Closing the door behind me, I thumb the business end of the Bic. The flame creates a small orange glow of light. To my right is a stone wall littered with graffiti from another, ancient time. I guess the language to be Latin, mixed with the occasional passage in Italian or French, along with some freakishly ancient dates like 1654, 1710, 1732, and a few more from the early nineteenth centuries. Some of the graffiti is carved into the wall rather than painted on.

It's impossible to stand upright.

People were shorter back in the fourteen hundreds.

With the glow from the Bic flame lighting the way, I keep moving through a corridor that angles gradually downward. It doesn't take me long to realize that not only am I walking inside a secret passage that's located inside the cathedral wall, but that it hasn't been traversed in a very long time.

The evidence is right under my feet.

Bones. A thigh bone here and a skull there. Tattered remnants of clothing. Rusted chains and shackles that hang from the stone walls in various places. The floor is soft under my shoes from moss and mold that's grown there over the years. The smell is organic. Like the moldy worm smell you get after a brisk rain.

The smell is death and decay.

I keep walking, for a time that seems to last far longer than it should, as if the cathedral has spontaneously doubled in size since I entered into the secret shaft. I can only imagine that the shaft not only served as a private portal but also as a place of torture for heretics. The Roman Catholics used to burn sinners at the stake right outside the cathedral doors. It only makes sense that they imprisoned them also.

Renaissance-era Christians: the conquerors of heaven, defenders of hell.

I keep heading down into the shaft, making a sharp right here and a gradual winding left there, until finally it levels off and the temperature cools noticeably, the sickly smell of ancient dead air dissipating. I walk the remaining few feet and eventually come to another steel door with yet another padlock securing it. I pull out the .9 mm and blow this lock away just like the first one.

Pushing the door open, I'm not exposed to the bowels of the cathedral. Instead, I find myself climbing a short flight of stone steps up into another building altogether. It's an empty space surrounded by eight stone walls. An octagon. It takes me a moment to gather my bearings, but soon enough I'm able to deduce that I'm inside the Rotonda di Santa Maria, another Brunelleschi building almost no one ever visits since it's located directly in the center of student housing. I only know about it because when I first came here, right out of college, I partied with some of the art students. We smoked cigarettes and drank wine right outside the rotunda on the stone steps.

So much for reminiscing about the good old days.

Back to the watch-your-ass-or-die days I've known so well as of late.

In the near distance, the sirens continue to blare, but not for me. For a big Russian who fell from the Duomo.

I check my watch.

Almost three in the afternoon.

Two hours before I'm to meet up with Lola. If memory serves, the Accademia is located not far from here, off the Via Guelfa. For a brief moment I think about hiding out there in the presence of Michelangelo's white marble statue of David, the Goliath slayer. But then I think better of it. I'm not here as a tourist, like I was my first time. It's possible my face has been broadcast to every security guard and cop in the city, even if they do somehow believe the dude who fell from the Duomo is their man. I've lost both my computer and my backpack and have no means of getting them back. Luckily I have my passport, wallet, cash, and smartphone stored inside the pockets of my leather jacket, or I'd really be in a fix. I also have my weapons. Soon as the authorities go through the stuff I left behind at the Uffizi, they'll realize the big spattered Russian is not me, and they'll begin an intensive search throughout the city.

The rotunda is currently empty and off-limits to tourists.

I remove the weapons from my pockets and place them in a far dark corner. I try one of the narrow exterior doors to see if it's bolted shut from the outside. Turns out it's not locked at all. No wonder I can make out dozens of empty wine and liquor bottles strewn all about the place in the rays of sun that leak in from the overhead louvers. The famous place has become a home for bums. Welcome to Renaissance reality. For now, anyway, the bums are nowhere to be seen. But I know they'll be back. For the present time, though, the joint is mine, all mine.

I take a seat beside my weapons, setting my right hand on the grip of the .9 mm should I require its services in a hurry. I press my back up against the stone wall, close my eyes. In my head I picture a small, white, naked, curly haired David kicking Goliath's giant ass.

CHAPTER 46

I must have fallen asleep.

Because when I wake up with a start, the daylight is mostly gone. The place isn't entirely dark, but dark is certainly filling it up fast. In one of the eight corners opposite me sits an old man. At least he looks old to me from where I'm sitting. My immediate reaction is to feel for all my weapons.

They're still there.

I stuff the .9 mm into my shoulder holster and the .22 into my coat pocket. The fighting knife gets re-sheathed.

The old man is drinking wine from a tall bottle.

"*Buona sera,*" I whisper, the soft sound of my voice echoing off the bare stone walls.

"*Sera,*" he whispers, after taking a deep drink off the bottle, wiping his mouth with the back of his hand.

Since that's the extent of my Italian, I ask him in English if he lives here.

He just shakes his head, which I take to mean, *I don't speak English.*

I stand, brush myself off, and check my pockets for loose change. I pull out a couple of euros, cross the length of the floor, and hand them to him.

"*Grazie*," he whispers, taking the coins in his free hand while stealing another pull off the bottle with the other.

"*Prego*," I answer.

I make another check of my watch.

Four forty-five in the afternoon.

I meet Lola in fifteen minutes. Our first meeting in nearly a year since she made the fatal decision to go off with her former lover and father of her now-deceased son.

Exploding bullets still ring in my ears. My left hand throbs from a sliced and diced pinky finger. Shards of crushed Duomo rooftop tile still stab my knees, chest, fingers, and palms. But it's the thought of Lola that sets my heart pounding.

For the narrowest of seconds I feel like asking the old man for a pull off the bottle. But then I get a good whiff of him and think better of it.

CHAPTER 47

It's begun to rain when I step outside onto the Via Guelfa. I pull the collar up on my leather jacket and take a right down the narrow neighborhood street, the soles of my boots slapping against the cobbles. Slipping into a corner bar I order an espresso, a pack of Marlboro Light cigarettes, and a new Bic lighter. A translucent red one. I drink the hot espresso from a little white cup while the attractive, middle-aged, blond woman behind the coffee bar stares up at a small LCD television that's mounted to the wall in a far corner.

While the rainwater drips off my leather jacket, I light a cigarette and glance up at the television. The scene being broadcast is all too familiar. A large man trying to balance himself atop the Duomo. A man dressed in black, who can't possibly balance himself because he's shot not in the collar like I originally suspected, but through the left shoulder. A man with a gun in his hand whose feet slip out from beneath him, whose body slides down the length of the Duomo until he drops like a sack of rocks to the cobbled pavement below.

I sip my coffee and smoke my cigarette and anxiously wait to see if there is any footage of me either standing atop the Duomo or traipsing across the cathedral ceiling. But thus far, anyway, nothing.

My hunch has turned out to be a good one. With the Russian goon and me dressed so much alike, he acted like my stunt double during his fall to his death.

I should be feeling good about his death. I should be elated that he bought the farm and I'm alive to watch it on television, knowing that the police are not looking for me. Yet.

But I'm not happy.

Maybe there's some truth to the notion that every man's death diminishes all of mankind, but my built-in, shockproof shit detector tells me this is more personal than that. Because of me, another man is dead. I don't care if he's trying to kill me first or if his intentions are to retrieve a flash drive that contains information that might potentially kill a massive number of innocent people. He's still a man, and I'm responsible for his death.

I've had a bellyful of killing. When will it ever stop?

In my mind I picture the seventh level of hell, and I see myself occupying a place of honor along with the other infamous men of violence. Men who lived by the gun and died by the gun. I'm no better than any of them.

Dante would have loved me.

I finish my coffee, set the cup back down into the white saucer. The little metal spoon makes a clinking noise when the cup brushes up against it. I set a ten-euro note onto the bar for the cigs, the lighter, and the coffee, and I motion for the blond woman to keep the change. All one euro of it.

I step back out into the darkness of an early Florentine night. The wet cobbled street takes on an eerie glow that reflects the light of the streetlamps as obscure white bulbs. The cigarette still burning between my lips, I pull up the collar on my leather coat and feel the light raindrops slap my face. Every one of them screams of loneliness. Every one of them bears the likeness of Lola.

My former lover turned fugitive.

CHAPTER 48

She's sitting at the bar to my left when I walk through the door of Harry's American Bar. Except for the bartender, she's alone. Her long dark hair is draped over her left shoulder, and the skin on her chiseled face is tan and rich. She's shed a couple of pounds since I last laid eyes on her, not that she needed to. But from what I understand about her present condition, she's been under a lot of stress lately.

When she turns to look at me, her big milk chocolate brown eyes melt into mine. As she crosses her black-booted legs under a brown leather miniskirt, I feel like the rainwater dripping down my cheeks could, in fact, be tears.

To my left is a picture window that contains the words "Harry's American Bar" in big gray block letters. Through the glass you can see the Victorian-era streetlamps that illuminate the red, common brick knee-wall that runs the length of the swift-flowing Arno. To my right is Lola, in her tights, turtleneck sweater, and thin brown leather jacket.

The barkeep is a distinguished middle-aged man in a white shirt, black bow tie, and matching trousers. He politely asks me what I'll be drinking. Jack Daniels, I tell him. Lola says she'll take the same.

The bartender tells me in perfect English that Jack is a fine choice on a cool, rainy evening like this one. But he has no idea just how cool things are around here, and quite possibly, how cold they might get.

I go to take the stool beside Lola's.

"Can we grab a table in the corner?" she asks. "Better not to risk being seen through the window."

She's right, of course.

"Sure," I say.

The bartender tells us he will bring our drinks to us.

She slips off the stool. When she passes by me on her way to the table, I get a quick whiff of her rose petal scent. It doesn't take a psychologist to tell you that smell can provoke profound memory.

In this case, it steals my breath away.

We sit down at the table and just stare at one another.

Finally, I work up the strength to make words. "You look good, Lo," I say. "Don't look like a kidnap victim to me."

"Whoever said that?" she asks, smiling, brushing back long, thick hair.

I'm slightly taken aback, as if she just reached out and gently flicked the tip of my nose with her index finger. My stomach constricts. I feel my pulse throbbing in my head and injured hand.

"My contacts in New York led me to believe you're being held against your will," I explain.

She exhales, sits back. "Do you have a cigarette?"

"Since when did you resume smoking?"

"Since my life went to hell."

I pull out the pack of Marlboros and hand her one as the barkeep brings the whiskeys in clear drinking glasses set on small white plates. He also sets out a small pitcher of drinking water, should we want to add some of it to the whiskey.

When he leaves I say, "Can you smoke in here?"

"It's Harry's," Lola says.

"Of course," I say, reaching across the table with my lighter and firing up her smoke.

I light one for myself and return the pack to my coat pocket.

"Which is it, Lo? You being held against your will or not?"

"Yes. I mean no. Or…yes, yes." She's smoking and nodding. "What I mean is, I came here of my own free will. Christian told me he was doing some business here with Interpol. That we would be here for some months. I desperately wanted to get out of the States and to forget about losing Peter and you, and I trusted my…my…significant other." Pausing, smoking. "It was only after a week of our stay here that I learned about the flash drive and his true reason for being here. That's when Clyne revealed himself." Her smoking hand begins to tremble. "They stand to make a lot of money. While risking the lives of millions of poor, poor people."

"Did you try to leave?"

"Immediately."

"He forced you to stay."

"Let's just say he keeps me on a short leash."

Now I begin to feel a slow burn building inside my chest. It's important that I keep my cool and stay calm. "Has he hurt you in any way? He hit you? Threaten you?"

She shakes her head. "No, nothing like that. It's more a matter of knowing what will happen to me if I try to leave."

"He'd kill you."

She smokes. "I believe he would," she says and exhales.

The burn, heating up. Heart racing. "How did you get out tonight?"

"I cornered him into an argument. Then I told him I needed to take a walk to cool off. He's used to my walks and even more used to our fights."

"He trusts you'll come back and not simply hop a flight out." A question.

"I've never given him reason not to trust me. Besides..."

She looks away, her hands still trembling.

"Besides what, Lo?"

"He'd come looking for me. And he would employ people here in the city to come looking for me. I'd never get beyond the train station."

"So you are a prisoner."

"Yes," she says. "And I hate Christian Barter's guts almost as much as I detest Dennis Clyne and what it is they are about to do."

"You mean sell the flash drive to the Iranians. Is that their true intention?"

She nods. "You've been informed."

"A source was provided for me. The provider lost his life in the line of duty to the same bunch of Russians who killed me once already in Albany."

"Yes, the Russians want their flash drive back. My late son, Peter, contracted with them, and they want their property."

Suddenly the acid burn that fills me blooms, like a switch has been flicked inside my brain. I reach out and take hold of Lola's forearm. Time to ask her the question of questions.

"Do you know where the flash drive is, Lo?"

She nods again, smokes.

"Can you lead me to it?" A surge of optimism dislodging the brick in my stomach.

"It would be extremely dangerous."

"I understand that. This whole place is dangerous. But it's something I have to do."

"For you? For the tragic mistake you made in handing it over to Clyne in the first place? Or for the FBI?"

"Both," I say. "And for us."

She stamps out her now-smoked cigarette. "There is no us," she whispers. "Not any longer."

It feels like a slap to the face. But it's also something I have to accept. "I'm taking you out of here," I tell her. "We'll grab the flash drive, get on the train, and then take the next flight out of here."

"Dick Moonlight, knight in shining armor. Well, Richard, aren't you just a little bit too late to be saving our relationship?"

"It's never too late."

"Is that how you reassured yourself when you cheated on me with Scarlet Montana? With the others?"

I feel my breath exit my lungs along with the cigarette smoke. "I have this condition, Lo—"

"I'm sick of hearing about that bullet, Richard. You have a conscience and a soul and they're perfectly fine. That bullet is and has been your crutch. Get over it."

"This the clinical psychologist speaking? Or Lola Ross? Excuse me...Lola Rose, your true last name. The name you hid from me for years. It's not like you're beyond deception."

"It's me in here, Richard. Just me. And I'm not going back to that life I lived with you." Turning away. "I'd rather take my chances here."

For a moment, we drink. I shoot my whiskey while Lola sips hers. I motion to the barkeep for another.

"Easy, killer," Lola warns. "It's ten euros a drink in this establishment. I hope the FBI provided you with some mad money."

"They want me to produce receipts when I make it back."

"*If* you make it back, you mean."

My second whiskey arrives. I sit and stare at it.

"I'll ask you again," I say after a time. "Will you leave Florence with me?"

A tear begins to fall down her left cheek. "Yes," she whispers. "I will leave with you. But I make no promises about us beyond that."

"Can you trust me for the time being?"

"Do I have a choice?"

"Can you take me to the flash drive?"

"I think I can."

"Now?"

Running her hands through her hair. "That's the question."

"You have to be sure," I say. "There's no room here for error. Clyne or Barter sees me, they'll kill me on the spot, dump me in the river, and no telling what they might do to you."

"It's Tuesday," she begins to explain. "There's an old gym located in the center of town. Ricciardi's Gym, run by a man who used to compete with Arnold Schwarzenegger. Barter and Clyne lift weights there on Tuesday and Thursday nights."

"Clyne?"

"You noticed how much weight he's dropped since he's been here? He's a health fanatic now. His psychological profile is now that of a free man intent on attracting a woman to help him enjoy what will be his newfound wealth. Ultimately, he's playing out a game of revenge against his cheating wife."

"God. Sounds like you've had the, uhhh, former APD dick on the couch."

"Passes the time. Especially when my heart is learning to hate as much as it used to love."

"How can you be sure they made their date at the gym tonight?"

She pulls out her cell.

I drink some more whiskey while she calls Barter.

When he answers she asks him how long he's going to be at the gym. Her voice is cold enough to frost over the North Pole. I recall that voice very well. Makes me feel good she's using it on Barter.

She hangs up. "We have approximately one hour to retrieve your precious flash drive," she informs.

I stand. "We've leaving," I say, peeling off thirty euros and sliding them under the empty drinking glass. "Now."

Lola gets up and begins to follow. "Just like old times," she says.

"Let's hope not," I say, holding the door for her.

CHAPTER 49

Lola's apartment is not far from here. Just a straight shot across the Piazza Santa Maria Novella in the direction of the train station. From there, we hook a right onto busy Nazionale. Lola follows close behind me, not saying anything, while we walk one in front of the other over the narrow sidewalk in the darkness and in the rain. When we come upon the Via Guelfa, which runs perpendicular to Nazionale, I stop and Lola takes the lead.

"It's just a few buildings in," she says, her voice showing signs of fraying nerves and maybe fear.

I reach into my leather jacket and thumb the safety off on the shoulder-holstered .9 mm. Then I say, "Let's do this, Lola. Let's get the hell out of rainy Florence."

"We have no other choice, Richard?" she says, and begins the long, short walk down the Via Guelfa.

Her apartment building is nondescript for Florence, in that it looks a lot like every other four- or five-hundred-year-old townhouse on the block. Five stories, old french windows protected by thick wood shutters painted lime green, Victorian-era metal lamps mounted to the stucco walls, the ground-level stucco walls marred by colorful graffiti shouting out political slogans and threats of anarchy.

Lola unlocks the door and we slip into the narrow tile-floored entry. She goes to flick on the overhead corridor lamps, but I grab hold of her hand.

"No," I whisper. "No light."

She heeds my warning and begins climbing a short flight of stairs.

Reaching into my coat, I slip out the .9 mm and follow.

The door leading into Lola's apartment is preceded by a landing that's made entirely of stone. It's so old it has a distinct list to it, making me feel like at any moment I might fall backward. The doors are thick wood french doors secured by a deadbolt with pulleys for openers. As is the custom in Italy, the landing outside the door also serves as a makeshift closet, housing a mop and a bucket, plus a broom and a couple of plastic bottles of cleaning solution.

It takes Lola a moment to negotiate the key in the lock in the semidarkness. Then I hear the distinct click-clack of a bolt being sprung and the squeak of a door being pushed open. We're in.

Lola flicks on a dull, wall-mounted sconce. She attempts to turn the overhead lights on, but again I tell her not to. One light will do.

A quick glance at the place reveals brick walls covered in new white stucco that in some areas has been removed to reveal some faded, ancient detailing, which I understand is the modern architectural norm for buildings considered historic. Ninety-nine percent of the structures in Florence probably make the historic cut. There are floor-to-ceiling bookshelves to my right and beyond that a small dining room with a kitchen on one side and a bath on the other. Behind me is a bedroom. To my right a couch that looks like it's been doubling as a bed. Clyne's bed, no doubt.

"Where is it?" I ask.

"In the bedroom," Lola answers.

"Show me," I say, feeling my heart sink at the thought of entering into the bedroom where my former lover sleeps with her new man.

The bedroom is rectangular and good-sized for an apartment, with thick wood beams supporting a stucco ceiling. The wall opposite the bed is brick and partially finished with white stucco. Same for the wall to my left.

There are two big french windows that are presently open, admitting the sounds from the street below. It's quiet, with only the occasional Mini and Vespa passing by or neighborhood dweller walking past on the cobbles in the steady rain.

The bed is a queen-sized futon. It hasn't been made, the sheets and covers scattered mostly at the foot of the bed like some serious wrestling went on here recently.

Wrestling...

I prefer to put the image out of my mind.

Lola kneels onto the bed, at the head where two sets of head-dented down pillows reside. There's a tall, almost life-size print of Botticelli's *Venus* that covers almost the entire wall above the bed. The naked, blond-haired beauty in the painting is floating in a big clamshell while angels blow wind gusts upon her from puckered lips and a handmaiden attempts to cover up her nakedness with a blanket. I never did get to see the real thing during my recent unpleasantness at the Uffizi, but I've seen maybe a dozen prints just like this one hanging on the dorm room wall of just about every college woman I ever dated.

Lola carefully lifts the framed print off the wall, revealing a recessed safe. She sets the painting onto the bed. The small safe opens not with a combination but a skeleton key. Sliding back off the bed, she lifts up the edge of the futon and uncovers the key. Replacing the mattress, she once more sets herself on her knees before the safe.

"That's it?" I say. "That's the extent of your security system?"

"It's not my flash drive," she answers.

She slides the key into the safe lock, twists it. The safe opens.

Reaching inside the dark space, she pulls out three American passports along with a couple of bundles of euros wadded together with rubber bands. Then she pulls out a .9 mm S&W, identical to the service weapon I used to carry as an APD cop, and two extra loaded ammo clips. The third thing she pulls out is the flash drive, which is protected in a little plastic Ziploc sandwich baggie.

For a moment, I stare at it. Then, realizing what it is and how important it is to some very bad people, I hold out my hand. "Please," I say.

Lola exhales, sets it into my hand.

The quiet of the rainy night is shattered by the deep voices of two men coming from directly outside the open windows.

CHAPTER 50

Lola's eyes go wide.

"It's them," she whispers. "They're early."

I shove the flash drive into the right-hand pocket of my leather coat.

We hear the front door to the building open and slam closed.

"What do we do?" she begs, sliding off the bed.

I hear the sound of footsteps coming up the stone stairs.

"They carry weapons on them?"

"Always."

"I'm not gonna shoot it out with them."

"I'll distract them," Lola says. "You sneak out the door. You have what you came for. Just go. I'll be fine."

"Sure, until they find out the flash drive is missing. You'll be lucky you don't end up in the river with your throat cut." I take hold of her arm. "I'm not leaving without you."

I hear the key entering into the lock on the front door.

"Greet your man at the door," I say, releasing my grip and snatching up the euros, the passports, the pistol, and the extra clips. I press my back up against the wall, out of sight of the open bedroom door. "Lead them into the kitchen and come back here to the bedroom for something you forgot. We'll just walk out the door together."

The front door opens.

Lola's lover is home.

CHAPTER 51

"You're home early," Lola says.

Barter bursts out in laughter. "You got a man hidden in our love den?" he jokes.

If he only knew.

"Very funny," she says. I can tell she's doing her best to keep her voice calm and without alarm.

"I'm thirsty as hell," remarks the voice of Dennis Clyne. "Whatta we got to drink?"

"I was just about to show you both something special in the fridge," Lola answers. "My little bubbly peace offering to you, darling. Come, it's in the kitchen."

"I should change, Lo," Barter comments. I hear him taking a step toward the bedroom.

"No!" Lola barks. Then, reining herself in, she says, "It'll only take a sec. Come on, hon, I've been waiting."

Hon, darling...

I think I'm going to be sick. I have to put the thought of them together out of my head, even if my eyes are staring at their bed and their pillows below the open safe.

The. Open. Safe.

From where I'm standing I can see that we didn't empty it out completely. There's something else inside it. Something reflecting the lamplight and that's stored in a plastic baggie, just like the flash drive in my pocket.

"Yeah, Agent Barter," Clyne says, "shoot your woman some slack, why don't you. Some bubbly sounds really good right about now."

Good old Clyne. Concerned about making a relationship work even when it's obviously over, just like him and his ex-wife. The woman who drove him to a life of international crime.

A pause ensues, as if Barter is weighing the pros and cons of his next move. My .9 mm is gripped in my right hand, barrel pointing up at the ceiling, safety off. Right now it's two against one. If the former FBI agent enters the room, I'll have no choice but to shoot him with the intent to seriously wound. That would level the playing field.

"Ah, what the hell," Barter says and exhales. "And don't call me agent, Officer Clyne."

Footsteps. Moving the opposite way, toward the kitchen.

That's when I make my move. I step over to the bed, place one knee upon it, and stuff my left hand back into the safe. I pull out the plastic baggie. There's a second flash drive inside it. A second flash drive identical to the first. I wonder why Lola wouldn't mention the presence of a second device. Perhaps she didn't know about it, or perhaps she didn't want me to know about it. No time to think things through right now. Time only to survive and make an escape. Me and Lola.

I stuff the second flash drive into my pocket along with the first, close the safe, and pull the painting back over it. Then I slide off the bed. With my back once again pressed up against the wall and the .9 mm at the ready, I get set to run out the door, soon as Lola makes her way back.

They've entered the kitchen, where I can hear them going through the refrigerator.

"Thought you had a nice surprise for us, Lo," Barter says.

"Oh crap." Lola grousing. "I forgot the best part. Don't move an inch, I'll be right back."

I hear her returning.

I move out from the bedroom wall.

She makes her way along the corridor until she's at the door. That's when I swing around, open the front door, and jump out, pulling Lola with me.

CHAPTER 52

I close the door as gently and quietly as possible. But the effort is wasted when the door closer engages, issuing a loud mechanical click-clack.

There comes a shout. "Hey! Lola!" Barter's voice.

Lola wasn't kidding. She is a prisoner in her own home.

In the corner is the mop bucket and mop. I pull out the mop, slide the wood handle through the two pulley openers. To the sound of footsteps running to the door, Lola and I bound down the short flight of steps and out into the street.

"Go, Lola!" I shout. "Don't look back."

"I'm already gone!"

They're both standing in the bedroom windows by the time we hit the street. I don't see their pistols but I hear the shots. The bullets ricochet off the wet cobbles, sending up bright orange sparks. I grab hold of Lola's hand tightly, sprint the length of the Via Guelfa, out of range of Barter's and Clyne's automatics.

The broom handle I stuffed between the door pulleys.

How long will it hold?

Probably not nearly long enough.

I go right onto Nazionale, gripping Lola's hand, pulling on her, dragging her around the tight corner just as a city bus is barreling its way through the intersection. The roads here, even the major ones, are so narrow the girth of the bus takes up the entire width of the one-way street. The sidewalks are even narrower, forcing me to release Lola's hand while we negotiate through the evening crowd of tourists and natives.

"Don't lose me, Lola!" I shout above the noise of the traffic, the now-driving rain running down my face and into my mouth.

"Just keep running!" she assures me.

We make it across Faenza and then out beyond an area where Nazionale widens, leading to the Piazza Santa Maria Novella to my left, and to the right the Santa Maria Novella train station.

Our destination. Our escape.

Lola and I enter the crowded art deco, Fascist-era station to the sound of locomotives pulling in and out of the many concrete platforms that service the transit hub that Mussolini built. The smell is acrid smoke and diesel fuel. The hum of people and machines is nearly deafening.

To our left is a giant room that houses the ticket booths. The lines are long and slow. I know that the train to Pisa and its international airport run every half hour, the ultimate destination along the route being not Pisa but Lucca, which is located along the coast. I also know that you don't have to wait in line at the ticket counter for a ticket. You can purchase them at any one of the many newsstands located inside the dark brown and off-white marble-finished building.

It's exactly what I do. Purchase two tariffa regionale Toscana tickets from the newsstand vendor for ten euros total. Tickets in hand, I peer up at the departures board. Lucca leaves on the hour in seven minutes on track eight.

Seven minutes.

An eternity when you're being chased by men who want to kill you. Men who are perfectly aware the only quick way out of Florence to Pisa is by train. I've been to this city three times now, and I know that taxis don't go there and buses take forever. That is, if they're even operating.

"Let's go," I tell Lola.

"We'll take the farthest car from the station," she suggests. "The one hooked up directly to the engine."

"All the way down the platform," I say.

"Let's just go. Now. Go. Now."

We move, sidestepping along track eight, steam slowly oozing out of the air brakes beneath the many baby-blue, single- and double-decker cars that make up the long, regional train. When we get to the final car behind the engine, I take a fleeting glance over my right shoulder. Barter and Clyne are nowhere in sight. But I doubt their absence will last forever.

A quick check of my wristwatch.

Four minutes until the train departs.

Four excruciatingly long minutes.

Just a few feet away from us, mounted on the thick pillar that supports the electronic destination marker, is the yellow validation box. All train tickets in Europe must be validated or the bearer will face a stiff fine or, in some cases, expulsion from the train. I slide the tickets into the designated slots, and the machine mechanically validates the tickets by stamping the date and time on them in blue ink. It's all that's needed for us to board.

We hop onto the train and depress the wall-mounted trigger that opens the sliding doors. Just a couple of people occupy seats at this hour of the evening. I wish there were more people for us to blend into. But it will have to do.

The doors close behind us.

We take two seats with windows that overlook a second set of tracks parallel to our own, not the concrete platform. We sit and listen to our hearts beat.

We count the seconds until we make our escape from Florence.

CHAPTER 53

We sit in absolute silence until we feel the pull and jolt of the slowly moving train. Lola grabs my hand, squeezes it hard. I look out the window opposite the aisle and watch the platform pillars begin to fly by as the train picks up speed.

When we're finally away from the station, Lola exhales in relief. "My God," she whispers. "We did it. We got away from them."

I squeeze her hand to reassure her. To let her know that I still love her. No matter what.

The car door slides open then, and Barter steps on through.

CHAPTER 54

No time to hide.

I manage to draw my automatic just a split second before Barter, get the jump on him as Clyne steps into the car behind him. Pistol poised before me, I slide out of my seat, stand four-square in the narrow aisle.

The black man seated four rows up from me is wearing headphones. His eyes go wide when he sees the gun. The middle-aged woman seated in the row behind him, only a few feet away from where Barter is standing, gets a look at my gun and screams.

Barter's wearing a waist-length black leather coat not unlike my own. He assumes a sly smile, starts sliding his shooting hand into its interior.

"Don't," I say, voice low, as even-keeled as possible. Then, focusing my eyes on both the black man and the woman seated behind him. "Go. *Vi*. Go. Leave!" They don't wait for me to ask a second time. They stand and exit the car without their bags, squeezing past Barter and Clyne as they do it.

The four of us are alone in the car. Beneath us the train sways along the tracks as it works up toward high-speed. Outside the window, quick visual snippets of the lush, lamp-lit Tuscan countryside. You can't see them in the dark, but I know that beyond the light are rolling green hills and pastoral landscapes filled with vineyards and fields of olive and fig trees ripe for the picking. You can see why people spend big bucks to spend time here. It's peaceful, serene, and as far removed from death as one place can possibly get on this earth. Except for me and Lola and the men facing my black gun barrel at the other end of the car, that is.

I thumb back the hammer on the automatic.

"Hands," I say. "The ceiling...both of you."

Reaching into my pocket with my free hand, I hand Lola the .22 revolver. It's not loaded, but they don't know that. "Hold this on Clyne's big fat face while I relieve them of their guns," I say.

I can't see her face, but somehow, I feel Lola smiling. "Happy to help out," she says.

I work my way up the aisle until I'm so close to Barter that I can smell the rain drying on his leather. I reach into his coat and pull out his automatic. Then I belt him over the head with it. He drops down into the empty seat directly beside him.

I take Clyne's weapon from him.

"There's no need to hit me," Clyne interjects. "I'll behave."

I give his suggestion some serious consideration and decide not to whack him.

"I believe you fucking will behave, Clyne," I agree, storing both of the weapons in my coat pocket.

"You have my flash drive," he adds. "I'd like it back."

"Not a chance."

"What can you possibly gain by having it?"

"Maybe I want the chance to sell it."

He smiles. "Not you, Moonlight," he says. "I pegged you for a bleeding heart right off the bat. You make a lot of wrong choices and decisions, but you wouldn't ever purposely do something wrong. Not something that would perhaps upset your position with God."

"You believe in heaven and hell, Clyne?"

He nods.

"Really," I say. "Interesting. So do I. I know firsthand what heaven looks like because I've been there."

He taps his temple in the spot where my botched suicide's scar protrudes from my skull. "Seems to me you've been to hell too," he says, that smile growing wider.

I picture myself seated at my kitchen table, a pistol barrel pressed up against my temple.

"Hell is where you find it," I say.

"Ain't that the truth," he says.

Commotion.

Coming from the opposite end of the car, in the space between the engine and the car where the toilet and additional storage is located.

"It's the ticket taker," Lola says.

I'm thinking, the ticket taker must have been inside the engine with the conductor. They are still called conductors, right? My gun still planted on Clyne, I quickly shoot a glance over my right shoulder toward the other end of the car. The uniformed man is standing inside the space, talking with someone on his radio. I know it's only a second or two before he enters the car and asks for our tickets.

I pocket my weapon along with the other two guns and tell Clyne to sit down beside his partner. "Just pretend he's asleep," I tell him.

"Sure thing, Mr. Moonlight," he says, not without a sly smile. "A man knows when he's beaten."

"Funny, Clyne," I say, backing to the other end of the car, next to Lola. I take her hand. "Forgot how funny you are. But I also know you don't want to go to Italian prison. That ticket taker recognizes you, you're done."

"Why not just tell the ticket taker who I am and be done with it?"

"Maybe I will," I fib, pulling Lola with me back up the car to them, slipping with her into the two seats one row up and across from theirs, keeping my pistol aimed at them at all times via the right-hand pocket on my leather jacket. "Just sit still and maybe I'll keep my mouth shut."

The door slides open.

"*Billeto*," says the small, mustached man to Lola and me.

I see Barter stir, coming to. There's a fresh pinky-finger-sized gash in his forehead.

I hand the tickets to the ticket taker. He checks to make sure they're validated and pokes holes in them with his hole puncher.

I turn to Lola.

"Get up," I say.

She does. I take hold of her hand and pull her back out into the aisle. We hustle rudely past the ticket taker, as he now hovers over Clyne and Barter. He issues a grunt like, *Fucking American tourists.*

I slap the wall-mounted door opener behind him. When it slides open, we slip out of the car and begin barreling our way car to car, to the opposite end of the high-speed train.

CHAPTER 55

"Why didn't you tell the ticket man?" Lola says from behind me as we switch cars. "This could be all over right now."

I'm listening to Lola's words, but I'm also looking out for the two people I chased out of the car. The black man and old woman who either are too frightened to alert authorities or have by now done so and it's only matter of time until this thing is all blown to hell.

"The little man carries a ticket punch, not a hand cannon, Lo. What's he gonna do, arrest them? Hold them at bay with the ticket punch? Take them into custody for us? Besides, you really wanna open up that can of worms?"

"Beats risking our lives."

"Say ticket guy calls in the Italian lancers, we give those two jerks up. We risk not only giving up the flash drive, but the both of us will be detained for who knows how long. It's not my business to have them arrested. My business is the flash drive and you. That's where it ends."

We keep moving through the brightly lit cars in the center of the train, keeping an eye out all the time for the passengers who fled, or the police or railroad security they might've beckoned. Then I feel the train slowing down. We're making our first stop along the route.

"Let's move to the coupling," I say to Lola.

She follows me through the sliding door to the cramped space between cars. There's no one else standing there. Peering through the glass doors, I see passengers getting off at the stop. Locals mostly, going home from work in Florence. But then I catch sight of two people being forced off the train by two uniformed men. They are railroad security. Ticket man's cavalry!

It's Barter and Clyne, and they are illuminated in a wide arc of sodium lamplight. Railroad security have their weapons drawn. No doubt they patted down the two amigos for weapons, but they wouldn't have found any since I'm carrying them in my coat pocket. I also realize it's possible that if the two people I chased out of the car earlier have alerted security about me and my gun, Clyne and Barter are likely taking the rap for it now. Maybe they witnessed only one man with a gun, but that doesn't mean that man didn't have an accomplice traveling with him.

Peering out the window at Barter and Clyne.

They're both arguing with the security guards, and one more man who has joined them. It's the little mustached ticket taker. He's holding up their two paper stubs. I don't need to hear what they're arguing about to know that they're being kicked off the train for not having validated their tickets and possibly for being suspected of brandishing a weapon or weapons.

Barter is holding a hankie to his head where I pistol-whipped it.

Clyne is trying not to look obvious as he scans the windows of the train cars for Lola and me. When a police car pulls up with its rooftop lights going outside the station and two *polizia* emerge and approach the two wanted men, I feel my body become lighter than air. My theories on why the two amigos have been kicked off the train are both right and wrong.

"They're being arrested," Lola observes. "All the time we've spent here. All this waiting. All this misery and risk. And it's not having validated tickets that gets them."

"Not paying attention to the little details," I say. "It'll get you every time. But that's not why they're being arrested."

"Confusion fills my head," she says.

"Not having validated tickets got them noticed by the ticket taker, but that's when their faces gave them away."

She nods, smiles. "He recognized them, didn't he?"

I nod.

"Interpol must have sent out alerts ages ago to be on the lookout for the two men and possibly even for you, which means that if that ticket taker and security get back on the train, I want you hiding your face for the rest of the journey."

She grabs hold of my hand, squeezes, like she's trying to tell me I can count on her.

The train starts moving again.

Slowly we make our way to where Barter and Clyne are being handcuffed by the police officers. As we pass, I catch both their sets of wide, angry eyes. I see Barter's narrow gash, swelled and stained with fresh blood. Smile painted on my face, I pull one of the two plastic baggies containing a flash drive from the coat pocket that doesn't house the weapons, waving it at them as we pass.

Arrivederci and fuck you too.

PART IV

CHAPTER 56

Lola and I land at JFK International later the next afternoon after managing to grab the last two available seats on a Delta flight leaving Pisa in the late morning. We slept almost the entire way, not saying much of anything to one another, mostly not wanting to confront the subject of "us" while crossing over the Atlantic.

Funny, but not once throughout the mostly bumpy flight was I concerned about crashing and burning. It was as if the presence of Lola back in my life, even if only a physical presence, seemed to suck the fear right out of me. Or maybe my sudden mastery over my fear of flying had more to do with being out of range of the numerous criminals who wanted to see me dead. They say flying is safer than crossing the street. Statistically speaking. But then, people do die while crossing the street. Even a quiet neighborhood street. It's just a matter of being in the wrong place at the wrong time.

As Lola and I flew through a crystal-blue sky over an ocean of snow-white clouds, I knew that we were both two people caught up in love at the wrong time. That wrongness nearly cost us our lives.

After we get through customs and immigration, I call Agent Crockett for a pickup.

"Let me get this straight," she says, noticeable shock in her voice. "You're in the United States, and you have the flash drive on your person. You say Barter and Clyne have been picked up by local police outside Florence. You're sure it's the right flash drive."

"They were picked up by the local cops, yes," I confirm, knowing that I have two identical flash drives stored inside my coat pocket. "I have *a* flash drive. Lola tells me it's the right one. I have only faith to go on."

"And Dr. Ross is with you."

"Affirmative. Why hasn't Interpol alerted you about Barter and Clyne?"

"Could be they don't want to alert me yet," she explains. "Welcome to the world of unshared intelligence."

Cloak and dagger...

Then she adds, "Stay put. I'm sending Zumbo out to get you. Don't talk to anyone, and try to avoid crowded areas. Maybe it will be best to grab a drink or something in a quiet airport bar, since it will take him the better part of an hour to get through traffic and to JFK. You have money, I take it?"

"Yes," I say. "We have money."

"Keep your phone handy. Zumbo will call when he's close."

"Roger that."

She hangs up.

I turn to Lola. She brushes back her long hair. We're both still wearing the same clothes from a couple of days ago. She looks beautiful, but I can see the exhaustion in her eyes and, I think, something else too.

Regret.

She might not be saying anything about it. But my built-in shit detector is picking up the vibes loud and clear enough. Or what the hell, maybe I'm just imagining things. It's been a long night. A long couple of days. Christ, it's been a hell of a long year.

"My contact suggests we have a drink together."

She works up a grin. "Sedation," Lola says with a resolve that borders on outright depression. "Sounds perfect."

Per my orders from above, we search for a nice quiet bar to while away the minutes until the Zump arrives.

CHAPTER 57

We take a corner table in the back.

I order a beer. Lola orders a pinot noir.

We sit in heavy silence until the drinks come. When they do, I take a long pull on the beer and Lola carefully sips the pinot.

"I'm sure you've been spoiled with Tuscan wines," I comment. It's supposed to be an icebreaker.

She cocks her head, exhales. "Let's get this over with," she says.

I nod. "OK. Why'd you do it, Lo? Why'd you go with him? Why'd you go back to Barter, knowing what he was capable of?"

"That's just the point," she says. "I didn't have the slightest clue as to what he might be capable of."

"Trust," I say. "You trusted him."

She slowly works up a nod. "Yes. I guess you could say I found something about him to trust while I..."

Her thought trails off, but I get her meaning well enough.

"A trust you couldn't find in me."

She turns away, looks at the faux brick wall of the airport pub. "Something like that," she goes on. "I never knew what to expect from you. Just which Richard Moonlight I was going to get. The one who loved me, or the one who would sleep with another woman and then blame the bullet in his head for it."

"It happened once, Lo. And we weren't exactly a tight couple at the time."

"But we weren't *not* tight, either."

There's no arguing with her, because she's right, of course. I had no business sleeping with Scarlet Montana, the wife of my former boss at the Albany Police Department. I had no right, because even though Lola and I weren't exactly committed at the time, most of my nights were still spent sleeping with her in my bed, even if we didn't allow ourselves to have sex. The whole thing with Scarlet was brought on by my acting as her best friend and confidant for a very brief period when we'd get together in the early evenings when her abusive husband, my former boss at the APD, was still at work. Back when I was still recovering from my botched suicide, searching for a new direction in my new life separate from the cops and my then newly divorced wife, Lynn. My sleeping with Scarlet was inevitable, but it was still a mistake since, technically speaking, I was with Lola and Scarlet was married.

A big, beautiful mistake.

But one that I'll regret for the rest of my days.

"But you felt you could trust Barter, even though you didn't know him, other than as teenagers who made a baby you gave up some twenty-five years ago."

She sips her wine again. I drink some more beer.

"Despite what you might think now, what I had with Christian in high school was not a flighty, immature, one-night stand. I loved him and he loved me. Yes, we were young, but he was my first real love and had things not gone horribly wrong, I might have spent my life with him."

I see the tears build in her eyes. I know how desperately she wanted to leave Florence and the danger she was mixed up in there. But I also sense that deep down inside, Florence wasn't all bad.

And then it dawns on me.

"You miss him, don't you?" I ask, the air leaving my lungs. "You fucking miss him? Even now? Even after everything that's happened? Jesus, Lo, you're killing me here."

She looks up at me. Looks me in my eyes as a single tear falls down her cheek. "I can't help it," she whispers.

"Even after he steals a flash drive holding secrets that could obliterate millions of souls and tries to sell it to the highest bidder."

She begins to cry. "I'm so sorry, Richard."

My phone vibrates inside my pocket, right beside my breaking heart.

CHAPTER 58

I press the phone to my ear.

It's Zumbo. "Welcome back, sweetie," he says. "You've done your country a great service."

"Cut the bullshit, Zump. I'm tired. Where are you?"

He tells me he's double-parked outside the Delta check-in counter at the pickup area. He wants me to hurry before a real cop comes along and tickets him.

"Just volunteer an autograph," I say.

"You kidding?" he says. "I used up the autograph thing with NYPD a long time ago."

"We'll be there in three minutes. Sit tight."

"Right on, sweetie."

I thumb End.

Lola and I emerge through the sliding glass doors out onto the sidewalk of the busy airport pickup area. Zumbo is there just like he said he would be, standing outside the passenger-side door that belongs to a black four-door sedan with tinted windows that just screams *COP!*

He's wearing that same loud Hawaiian short-sleeved shirt over a pair of baggy blue jeans, even though it can't be much over forty degrees outside, and cloudy. It's unbuttoned halfway down his tight beer belly so that the butt of his automatic is exposed. As usual, he's sporting a four-day salt-and-pepper facial growth, not to mention a serious case of bed head.

"You've never looked prettier, Zump."

"Let me get your luggage," he says with a smile. "Oh, you don't have any. Silly me."

He opens the back door for Lola.

"You must be the infamous Lola," he says as she gets in, and he quickly closes the door behind her. Then, opening the front door for me, he says, "Brains before beauty."

I slip on in.

The door closes behind me and the cold steel of a pistol barrel presses up against the back of my head.

CHAPTER 59

"Did I tell you 'Welcome home' yet, sweetie?" Zumbo says as he pulls the sedan out onto the airport road.

I'm trying to get a look at who exactly has the gun pressed to my head. But my angle in the front passenger seat won't allow it.

"You OK, Lo?" I ask.

"For someone staring down a pistol barrel," she says. "I thought these were supposed to be your friends."

"Shut up your faces," says a man behind me. "Both of you."

I recognize the voice. It's low and gravelly. It's angry. It's in pain because of a shot-away kneecap. It's Russian-accented. It's Boris. He must have made it back to the States on an earlier flight. Out the corner of my eye I catch sight of another man, who's dressed in black leather like Boris. He's seated up against the far door, and he holds an automatic on me while Boris drags Lola over his lap and stuffs her between the two of them in the backseat. Boris returns his gun barrel to the back of my head, and his pal trains his on Lola.

"We all set back there?" Zumbo pipes up, beaming into the rearview. "Everybody warm and cozy?"

"Nice friends you got there, Zump," I say. "How much they paying you to sell out?"

"More than you can imagine, buddy," he answers. "More than my NFL pension, anyway."

Zumbo is happy as hell. He's even humming a song while tapping out the beat onto the steering wheel as he pulls out onto the Van Wyck Expressway in the direction of Manhattan. I know the song. It's Buster Poindexter. "Hot, Hot, Hot." Fuck. Now I'm gonna have the song in my head the whole ride long.

"What about Agent Crockett?" I ask. "She in on this shit too?"

"Normally I'd tell you to mind your own beeswax," Zump says in between verses of "Hot, Hot, Hot." "But since you and the missus back there don't have a whole lot longer to live, I might as well tell you that cute little Agent Crockett is not, I repeat, *not* a part of my most excellent relationship with my Russian friends here." He pauses to tap out some more *"Hot, hot, hot"s.* "You see, sweetie, one more mouth to feed would simply cut into my cut. I need to maximize my monetary potential instead of simply giving away the farm." Winks at me. "'Sides, I don't think she'd be into it anyway. Crockett is a Goody Two-Shoes."

"You don't say," I say, picturing the few short hours I spent in bed with her. "Congratulations."

He turns to me with one of his all-teeth smiles, slaps me so hard on the thigh it feels like a compound fracture. "Hey thanks, Moonlight," he bellows. "You know, I like you. Under different circumstances we might have been pretty good pals. Or more, even."

Or *more,* even?

"I just want you to be clear on what's happening here. You and the missus are buying the farm in the interest of security and my overall plan. You realize, of course, that it's strictly business."

"I understand, Zump. No harm done. Shoe could easily be on the other foot."

He slaps me again. A backhand to the sternum. It rattles my rib cage *and* my fillings. "You see that, Boris?" he barks into the rearview mirror. "Now that's some fuckin' A-1 Americana class for you, my commie Ruskie bro. *That's* how you go out. Not screaming like a girl to some crippled asshole like yourself to spare your pathetic little life. But with real dignity. Real, made-in-America pride."

I feel the pistol pressed harder against my head. "Do not call me Boris," says Boris to Zumbo. "This motherfucker," he says, cracking the muzzle against my skull, "he calls me Boris when he shoots off my kneecap. Boris is not my name, *da?*"

"Hey, Boris," Zump says. "Tell it to somebody who gives a shit. Far as I'm concerned, Reagan should've nuked your entire beet-eating outhouse of a country when he had the chance."

I feel Boris's hot breath on my neck. He flicks my earlobe with the barrel and leans forward.

"First I shoot both your kneecaps off," he whispers into my ear. "Then I rape your woman…while you watch, *da*? Then after I have shot cum inside her pussy and blown her pretty brains all over the ground, I'm going stick pistol into your mouth. When I am ready, I will make you pull trigger. From what I hear, you already know how to shoot self in head, *da?*"

I'm listening to Boris, but I'm looking out onto the crowded Belt Parkway that's taken over from the Van Wyck. With every word he speaks, with every bit of spittle that sprays against my ear, with every micro-ounce of rotten-garbage-like halitosis vapor that passes by my nostrils, the rage inside of me builds like a volcano about to erupt. It's just a matter of controlling it, and releasing it when the opportune time arrives.

It. Will. Arrive.

Zumbo doesn't take the turn for the FDR that runs along Manhattan's East River. Instead he passes over the Robert F. Kennedy Bridge and onto the Deegan for the ride north toward Albany. In the meantime, I'm trying to get a better look at the second man sitting in the back, his piece aimed at Lola's liver. The quiet one. I'm also trying to get a look at her. She has hardly spoken a word since we left the airport. I know she must be frightened out of her mind. But I need to see her to make sure she's OK. I need to see him to get an idea of what I'll be dealing with.

That's when I get an idea.

"Hey, Zump," I say. "It's cool, I been calling you Zump? Listen, man, I know time is short and all, but I gotta tell you, if I'm gonna buy it, I'd like to do it with an empty bladder."

"You can hold it, I think."

"Well, there's a little more to it than a simple wee-wee, I gotta say. And it wouldn't be very pleasant. How can I put this delicately?"

"You can speak your mind, Moonlight," Zumbo says. "We're all friends here. Well, maybe not Boris and Mr. Personality back there. But the rest of us are."

"Fuck you, Mr. Zumbo," Boris says, jabbing me once more with the pistol. When he says "mister," it comes out sounding like a snake: "Meeessster."

"It was a long plane ride," I say, "and it's a brand-new day, and well, Mother Nature calls."

Zumbo nods. "I get it. Gotta poop, don't ya?"

"Can't get one past you, Zump. You're too sharp."

"That's what some dipshit told me after I paid him ten grand to pilfer the final exams at Quantico. That I might have actually passed the tests without cheating. But I didn't want to take that chance."

"I agree. You would have aced them without having to cheat, Zump. But it's good to have a contingency plan in place. Smart thinking." A sigh, and a pained squirm in my seat, like I'm desperately trying to hold in Mother Nature. "So whaddaya say, Zump? How do I spell relief here? Trust me, I'm not planning anything other than guaranteeing you and our international friends a clean, shitless ride. So to speak."

Zumbo laughs. "Tell you what, Moonlight," he says. "Since you're so mature about this whole dying thing, I'm gonna stop at the next rest stop and allow you to pinch one final long, curly, satisfying loaf. How's that sound?"

"Jeez, thanks, Zump. It'll make for easy cleanup later on when I'm finally gone too. If you get my meaning."

He laughs again. "Yup, no one likes picking up a stiff with shit in his drawers."

Up ahead on the right is a sign for the next rest stop. It's ten miles away.

Ten miles for me to make a plan so that Lola and I can live and Zump and company can die horrible, painful deaths.

CHAPTER 60

We drive in silence.

Until Zumbo slaps the steering wheel. "Well I'll be dog-goned," he says. "All this time I never thought once about asking you for the flash drive. Can you believe that, Boris? I never even asked once. But then, neither did you. You soccer-loving pussy."

The barrel jabs the back of my skull once more. "I thought of asking for fleshy box," Boris grumbles. "Just assume we take it off him when he is dead." Perking up. "And my football is not pussy galore. It is hard man's sport." Laughing. "No helmets or padding to ease pain, *da*?"

"No helmets, no tackling, no scoring more than three lousy points a game," Zump points out. I can't help but think how right he is, despite our circumstances. Then he adds, "I think it's best to grab the zip-thingy now. Makes things easier." Holding out his right hand, palm up. "Let's have it, sweetie."

I begin digging in my coat pocket. I feel one of the two plastic baggies. I feel something else too. My cell phone. The ringer is turned off. Only the vibrator is on. They never took it off of me when I got in the car. I pull out one of the baggies and drop it onto the floor by my feet. On purpose.

"Silly me," I say and exhale.

When I twist and bend down to retrieve it, I can see that Mr. Personality is a small, thin man with a shaved head. He's got little cancer whiskers wrapped around his tiny little lipless mouth that are supposed to serve as a chin beard and mustache. His eyes are glass and his face tighter than a snare drum, the skin pale. I've seen killers in prison, stone-cold killers, and that's exactly who Mr. Personality reminds me of. Someone who can kill you slow with a knife and maybe enjoy a nibble on your flesh in the process. He's holding an automatic on Lola, who's been gagged with a big white handkerchief. No wonder she hasn't had anything to say.

I pick up the flash drive and hand it to Zumbo. "All yours," I say.

We pass a sign that says three miles until the rest stop.

"Just hold it another couple minutes, sweetie," Zumbo says, pocketing the flash drive into the chest pocket on his Hawaiian shirt. "Bet you're seriously turtling that loaf."

"It's a sure test of my potty training," I say.

We pull into the rest stop. It's one of those places that features a McDonald's as the main restaurant and a greasy chain pizza joint as a healthier alternative. Zumbo pulls into a spot at the back of the lot. Sneaky.

He kills the engine.

"OK, here's the deal," he says, turning his big body to face us all. "I'm gonna take Moonlight into the crap house. And so we don't have any other little side trips, Boris, you and Mr. Personality get to take the little lady to *her* bathroom. Maybe you can try and pinch one too, honey."

"What about following woman into crapper?" Boris says. "Can't simply walk in ladies' crapper." He says "what" like "vhat."

"No windows or exterior doors on these bathrooms, I happen to know. She's not going anywhere. And anyway, she's not out in three minutes, I'll go in after her myself since I'm a bigshot federal agent and you're just a commie with a bad knee, *capice*?"

"*Capice*...what is *capice*? Polish?"

"No, it's Italian, you stupid fucking soccer-loving one-kneed commie Ruskie. Now let's get moving. I don't have all day. We have a couple executions to attend, not to mention a double burial of sorts."

Zumbo opens his door and shifts his big weight out onto the parking lot. I get out and so do Boris and Mr. Personality, pushing Lola out before him.

"I don't think I have to remind you to behave, sweetie."

"You don't, Zump. A man knows when it's time to call it a life. Especially me." Making like a pistol with my right hand, pressing extended index finger against the scar on my temple. "I just want to enjoy one final constitutional."

He sets his gargantuan hand on my shoulder, pinches it, lovingly. A little too lovingly. He smiles, tells me to go on ahead of him. He wants to watch me walk with my cute little butt cheeks pinched tight.

Well I'll be dipped in shit. The Zump...the big football player...the macho New York Giant...he really is a fairy.

I toss him a wink. "I'll try, sweetie," I whisper.

CHAPTER 61

The rest stop is crowded with weekend travelers trying to get in some late-season fall foliage gazing. So is the men's room. Zumbo heads straight to an unoccupied wall-mounted urinal.

"Take care of business, Moonlight," he says to me while pulling himself out and producing a steady flow that spatters against the porcelain. "Just remember, I'm right here watching. Or listening, anyway."

I locate an empty stall and close the door behind me, securing it by turning the bolt. I don't bother with slipping off my coat, nor do I pull down my pants and attempt to appease Mother Nature. I just sit myself on the toilet seat while reaching for my cell phone inside my coat pocket. I start in on a text to Agent Crockett.

Zumbo and Russians kidnap us. Going to kill us. On Northway 87 above NYC. Ramapo. GPS this number.

I thumb Send.

I know it's silly to wait for an immediate reply. I'm also hoping they have an automatic GPS set up for the cell. It's an FBI-issued mobile phone, after all. How can it not be traceable? I know it's only a matter of a few seconds before Zumbo's big fat head peers down at me from over the side of the stall. I listen to the men and boys coming and going from the men's room, the sound of toilets and urinals flushing, sink faucets spilling water, hands slapping the wall-mounted hand dryers, the jet-plane-like sound of the hot air spewing out the stainless-steel nozzle.

Through the narrow half-inch opening between the stall door and the partition closer, I spot three huge, beer-lubed, blue-and-red New-York-Giants-jersey-wearing fans peeing in the urinals. Must be a special Thursday night game on the NFL Network. All three of them are shooting Zumbo these glances like they recognize him. And maybe they do.

I know I need to do something, but I have no idea what.

Until I see the bit of discarded newspaper lying on the floor a few feet in front of me.

"MAN PULLS GUN ON PASTOR DURING SUNDAY SERVICE!" reads the headline.

It comes to me then like a gusher erupting from my insides.

"You fall in, sweetie?" Zumbo barks. "You got a date with the devil, don't forget."

"On my way, Zump," I say, standing. The toilet flushes electronically despite my not having used it. Opening the stall door, I step on out and face the football fans.

"*GUN!*" I scream.

CHAPTER 62

In a word, the place goes berserk.

Most of the men run for the exit. But the three Giants fans stand their ground, zip up, step away from the porcelain urinating fixtures, and line up like they're linebackers and I'm the littlest Dallas Cowboys quarterback in the business.

"Not me!" I scream. "Him!" I point to Zumbo. "Look! He's got the fucking gun!"

They turn to him. Zumbo's holding an automatic in his beefy hand. They're not mistaking him for a football great now.

Zumbo's face is a mask of anger and violence. Doesn't matter how big he is or that he's armed. They fearlessly set themselves side by side, form-tackle position—knees bent, shoulders cocked, eyes wide and unblinking.

"Go for the knees!" I scream. "He's got bad knees!"

Zumbo raises up his automatic like he's about to shoot his way out of a perfect goal-line defense, instead of plowing through it with head, shoulders, and thrusting legs. The three Giants fans don't wait for him to shoot. Acting like a well-trained defensive unit, they gang tackle the former fullback, sending him careening back against a sink and a mirror, shattering both. He fumbles the automatic and it drops to the tiled floor. I jump into the scrum, snatch up the gun, and coldcock his bulbous head. He's out like a light with both eyes wide open. Or maybe I killed the motherfucker.

"You boys hold him right there," I tell them. "Damn shame too. Another pro football player turned to the dark side."

Right beside me is the janitor closet, the door to which is wide open. As if divine Providence were looking down upon me, there's a roll of gray duct tape sitting out on a shelf, along with dozens of rolls of commercial-grade toilet paper. I grab the tape and hand it to them. But before they go to work on him, I reach into his chest pocket, pull out the flash drive, and stuff it back into my coat pocket along with the other flash drive.

"Call 911!" I shout before exiting the bathroom for the ladies' room.

Out in the main lobby of the building, women and girls are running from the ladies' room. People are racing for the doors. The sound of breaking glass can be heard above the screams in the ladies' room. When I slip inside, I see Boris and Mr. Personality kicking in the doors on the stalls. They turn and look at me as I enter into the brightly lit restroom.

On cue they raise up their weapons.

I raise up mine.

No one shoots.

I shift my aim from Boris to Mr. Personality and back again.

No one's saying a word.

When the first cop enters into the bathroom behind me, I drop to my knees. Two exploding rounds take out the cop. I fire from down on my knees and nail Boris in the thigh, just above the place where I disintegrated his kneecap almost a year ago. He goes down on his ass.

But Mr. Personality has kicked open the last stall door, dragged Lola out by her hair, and jammed the barrel of his pistol against the side of her head.

I drop Zumbo's automatic and raise up my hands. "Don't hurt her," I say.

"I won't," Mr. Personality says, raising his first smile since they kidnapped us earlier. "First, I wish to make her my bitch, *da?*"

CHAPTER 63

We exit the ladies' room.

Boris shoots off a couple of rounds for effect. The deafening rounds reverberate inside the lobby, and the people who remain inside the building hit the floor. There's a cop standing directly outside the side entrance. He's using his radio, no doubt calling for backup. Boris hobbles through the first set of automatic sliding glass doors and shoots the cop in the head through the plate glass of the second set. Un-fucking-lucky cop.

Parked up along the curb is the cop's blue-and-white cruiser.

Boris limps toward the open door and the dash-mounted radio that's spitting out chatter about a SWAT team on its way. Raising his automatic, he pumps two rounds into the radio. Then he pulls the short-barreled riot shotgun from its housing between the bucket seats and grips it in his free hand.

"We need a car," Boris spits, his face pale, blood dripping down his leg. "Something fast and big."

He yanks on Lola's hair. She winces in pain.

"I'm going to kick you in the balls when this is over," she snarls.

Overhead, the sound of choppers arriving on the scene.

"How about the cop car?" I suggest, my hands raised over my head.

"No, motherfucker," Boris answers, slapping me upside the head with the pistol barrel. "It will be equipped with LoJack. They will follow."

My head grows light and the sharp pain seeps into my brain. Not now. Not. Fucking. Now. I concentrate with all my might, as if I can will the bullet in my brain not to press up against my cerebral cortex. Down and out I'll go. I need to keep my shit together for Lola.

Mr. Personality extends his pistol hand and points to a full-sized, white Ford Bronco that's being gassed up. "White Bronco!" he shouts.

"Just like O.J.," remarks a smiling Boris. "Mr. Juice."

The choppers are closing in, along with a train of screaming cop cars racing north along Highway 87. I'm hoping they get here before we make it to the Bronco. I'm also hoping that Crockett got my text and is planning our rescue.

Boris, in all his pain, cracks a smile. "Let's do it," he says. "Go! O.J.! Go!"

Stupid fucking Russians.

We race for the white Bronco.

CHAPTER 64

There's a typical dad gassing up the vehicle, not the actual soccer mom. The gas pumps are located a pretty good distance from the rest stop building, but the scene is nonetheless surreal. The dad is gassing up despite the obvious emergency going down in the very near distance. People are stubborn. People live in denial. He's midthirties, dressed in pressed Levi's, a yellow crewneck sweater under a Windbreaker. Taking the family out for a nice week of foliage watching up in the Catskills. It was probably hard to get time off from the office. Nothing's going to stop him or ruin his plans. Until now.

"Grab your family and run!" I scream, just seconds before Boris turns and whacks me once more with the pistol barrel.

"Fuck up, Moonlight!" he shouts.

My head rings. "It's *shut* up, Boris. *Shut* up!"

The driver tosses us only a glancing look. Two leather-clad Russians wielding weapons are coming at him, holding a woman hostage by the hair and another dazed and confused head case at gunpoint, and Soccer Dad keeps on fueling.

"Fucking *run!*" I shout out again, for which I receive yet another blow of the gun barrel.

This time it does the trick.

The dad opens the door on the Bronco's backseat, yanks a child into his arms while his wife exits the passenger seat screaming. All three run for the patch of green that separates the highway from the rest stop gas pumps.

To the sound of choppers on the horizon, Mr. Personality shoves Lola into the backseat and forces me to sit up front with Boris, who, despite the deep thigh wound on his leg, insists on driving. Without bothering to return the hose to the gas pump, Boris fires up the engine and peels out. In the side mirror, I can see the hose snap off at the metal coupling, sending out a burst of sparks that ignite the pump and the excess fuel that's leaked all over the pavement.

As we near the on-ramp the fuel catches fire and flashes. The entire island of pumps explodes, rocking the Bronco and sending the already panicked bystanders flat on their bellies.

"Van Damage." Mr. Personality chuckles, poking me in the head with the pistol barrel. "We are badass motherfuckers. Say it, Moonlight. We are badass motherfuckers."

Then, turning to Lola.

"You say it too, bitch...badass motherfucker."

"Fuck you," Lola says through clenched teeth.

"Just do it, Lo," I say. "Badass motherfucker. That's what you are, Mr. Personality."

"You can learn from boyfriend," Mr. Personality says. "But right now, I am boyfriend, *da?*"

I turn enough to see into the backseat through the corner of my left eye. Mr. Personality is trying to raise up Lola's skirt with the pistol barrel, while he's groping her left breast with his free hand.

She spits in his face.

He slaps her and resumes his groping.

That's when the Bronco locks up, sending us all careening forward.

"Stupid fuck!" shouts Mr. Personality at Boris. "Why you stop on highway?"

Cars and trucks blare their horns and swerve around us. I'm bracing myself for a severe collision.

"We did not think to retrieve flash drive from Zumbo!" Boris screams, while throwing the Bronco into reverse. He's backing the vehicle onto the soft shoulder. He's proceeding to make a three-point turn while occupying the right lane on a major highway packed with all manner of vehicles doing anywhere from sixty to ninety per.

I look down at Boris's leg.

It's soaked with blood. His face is pale. He's not thinking clearly. But then, he's right. They forgot all about the flash drive.

They also have no idea it's in my coat pocket.

He turns the opposite way onto the right lane and guns it.

That's when I see the tractor trailer heading straight for us.

CHAPTER 65

Boris steers to the right.

The confused truck operator steers to his left.

We're heading directly for one another.

"Fuck!" Boris shouts. "Fuck! Fuck! Fuck!"

He steers left.

The trucker steers right.

Still heading for one another.

"Take foot off gas, stupid motherfucker!" screams Mr. Personality.

Boris might be trying to remove his foot. But his thigh is shot through. He's got the pedal to the heavy metal as the Bronco races at the semi. Boris knows he's about to die because he closes his eyes and throws his hands up over his face.

"Lola," I say, turning. "Get down. Go flat onto the floor."

She does it. Mr. Personality doesn't quite seem to care. He looks like a deer caught in the headlights as the truck and the Bronco prepare to kiss grilles.

That's when I grab the wheel from Boris, yank it counter-clockwise, fishtailing the back end of the Bronco directly into the semi's front grille.

CHAPTER 66

There's an explosion. The shattering of glass and the crunch of metal against metal. I'm tossed around on the floor of the Bronco like the little steel ball inside a can of spray paint. Time moves especially slowly during an automobile accident. It's like one of those old grammar school reel-to-reel projectors slowed down so that events occur frame by frame instead of in one quick linear event.

There's the collision with the semi.

The hard-left snapping/spin fishtail motion of the Bronco.

The tossing of my body up against the underside of the dash.

My going in and out of consciousness, knowing that I may never wake up from the darkness once it overtakes me.

My trying to reach out for Lola, but knowing it's impossible...

My. Reaching. Out.

My blacking out...

CHAPTER 67

When I come to, there's sunlight shining on my face and the smell of acrid smoke filling my nostrils from a tire that's on fire not far from my head. I slowly come to realize that the Bronco has been split in two, as if a giant hand had picked the vehicle up and torn it in half like a white business envelope instead of two tons of metal, glass, and plastic.

I see that Boris is still strapped into his seat, the steering wheel impaled into his chest. His eyes are wide open. Staring down all eternity. Staring into the seventh level of violent hell.

I drag myself from the wreckage and crawl along the road the few feet to where the back half of the Bronco is located. Beyond it, Lola is lying on the road, having been ejected from what's left of the back portion. She's not moving. She's staring straight up at the bright sky, a trickle of blood running down her right cheek from out of her left eye.

I crawl toward her, trying to say her name. But I'm not able to make any words. My throat feels as if it's on fire, my lungs filled with concrete. At last I'm able to reach out and touch her left foot—but that's when a hand grabs my jacket collar and yanks me onto my back.

Mr. Personality is looking down on me.

There's a small laceration in the center of his forehead. Or maybe a hole, since a combination of blood and clear fluid is leaking from it. I squint to get a good look and decide that if I could stick my index finger inside it, I would touch his brains. He doesn't seem the least bit affected by the injury when he raises up his gloved fist, brings it down hard onto my mouth. He rears back and punches me again, the back of my head slapping against the pavement. I'm seeing flashes of blackness, and I sense I'm going to pass out again if I don't try to move myself.

When he cocks back his fist for another punch, I suck in a blood-tinged breath and roll out from under him. His fist slams the ground, causing him to shriek. I find a piece of metal, some shattered length of tough rod, lying a few feet from me. I snatch it up and jam it into the side of his neck. He stops screaming then. For a moment he goes perfectly still, like the rod sticking out of his neck isn't hurting him but empowering him all the more. Reaching into his leather jacket, he pulls out a knife handle and thumbs the switch that produces a blade.

"Moonlight dies now, *da*?"

He says it like he's offering me a hot cup of coffee.

Raising up the blade with both hands gripped around the hilt, he's about to thrust it into my heart when the little hole in his forehead expands and explodes, taking the back of his cranial cap along with it.

Mr. Personality falls dead on top of me.

I don't stop to ponder the mystery of his spontaneously exploding head. I push his deadweight body off me and go to Lola.

By now I'm aware of the sirens and the uniformed police surrounding the site of the crash. But I don't care about that. I need to get to Lola.

I manage to get up on my hands and knees. I go to her.

She's still lying on her back. She hasn't moved an inch since I first laid eyes on her after the crash a few moments ago.

"Lola," I say, kneeling over her. "Lo, can you hear me?"

But she's not responding.

I place my left cheek over her mouth and I don't feel warm air coming from her lungs. She's not breathing.

I straighten up my back, press the heels of both palms against her sternum, press down hard. I do this two or three times, until I reposition my face over hers and lock onto her mouth, forcing air into her lungs. Then I move back to her sternum, which I begin to punch as hard as I can, trying to shock the heart. Trying to make it alive again. Trying to bring Lola back.

Until I hear a voice from behind me say, "She's gone, Mr. Moonlight. I'm so very sorry."

I stop punching, and I feel the tears fill my eyes. The tears cloud Lola's face. They run into my mouth. I want to speak to her, say something, but I can't say anything. I can't make the words to tell her how much I love her and how sorry I am for everything.

A hand on my shoulder.

"Take a moment, Richard," says the soft voice of Agent Crockett.

I feel the air leave my lungs and my throat constrict. I feel my heart pounding in my chest, and it takes on an unbearably heavy weight.

Leaning into Lola, I close both her brown eyes with a trembling hand, then kiss both lids. I place my lips to her face and I taste the blood that stains it. Then I press my mouth against hers. For what will be the last time on this earth, I embrace her lips with a kiss.

A cold breath escapes my lungs. I wipe away my tears with the back of my hand. I force myself onto my knees, and then onto my feet. I steal one last glance at Lola. At her body. At her face. At her memory. Turning away from my one true love, I begin to make my way toward the sounds of sirens and the vision of flashing lights.

I feel nothing.

CHAPTER 68

I'm sitting in the backseat of Agent Crockett's ride. She's in the front passenger seat, her entire body shivering like she's freezing to death in sunny, seventy-plus-degree weather. Indian summer. I'm smoking a cigarette while she sips from a cup of hot tea to which she's added a shot of brandy from an emergency fifth she stores in the glove box of the big black suburban. From what she's told me, it comes in handy when she has to discharge her weapon at a live human being, like she did when she fatally shot Mr. Personality.

"How many people have you killed?" I ask her after a time.

"Including our Russian friend?" she answers. "Three. And each of the other two gave me the shakes for hours afterward. So we'll just sit, if you don't mind."

I stare out the window onto the scene. The crushed Bronco, the three bodies covered with rubber sheets, the disabled semi. Its blue-jeaned operator is being interviewed by both the cops and a guy in a suit who arrived on the scene in a car with the word "Progressive" painted on the side panel.

"I've killed more than I can count," I say after a pregnant beat. "At the time, I thought they deserved it. But I'm not so sure anymore."

"If they were going to kill you first, you had no choice."

I nod, smoke. "Maybe," I say, exhaling a stream of blue smoke. "I nearly killed myself once, and I'm still here. I let myself live."

I follow up with a laugh. But there's nothing funny in this. I believe in heaven and I believe in a hell. I've seen myself in hell in my dreams and I just can't shake the image.

"That's the important thing," Crockett softly speaks. "That you lived. And you've done good things, Mr. Moonlight. You've saved lives."

I glance at the body bags.

"And killed Lola in the process," I whisper.

"Lola made her own decisions," Crockett says. "She alone chose to go with Barter. No one made her go with him. She made the decision to enter into his life, not you. Lola would still be alive if not for her decisions, Mr. Moonlight. You have to believe that or it will weigh on you forever."

I smoke silently.

"Doesn't make me feel any better about anything," I offer after a beat.

"If you felt good about anything today," she says, "I'd say you weren't the least bit human."

I toss my still-lit cigarette out the window, watch as it sparks against the pavement. "We done here?" I say.

She nods.

I open the door, slip my left leg out.

"Oh, there is one more thing," Crockett calls out. She holds out her left hand, palm up.

I know what she wants even before she says the words. But I want to hear it from her mouth anyway.

"The flash drive," she says. "You do have it, don't you?"

For the briefest of moments I consider revealing the presence of two identical flash drives on my person. But what the hell, I'll give her one of them and see what happens. Who knows, perhaps one of them is a decoy and the other is the real deal. I have a fifty-fifty chance of walking away with the moneymaker.

Lola's dead now.

What the hell have I got to lose that hasn't already been ripped away from my chest cavity?

I reach into my coat, hand her one of the two plastic-bagged flash drives.

"Thanks," she says and nods. "You've done your country proud."

"Wow," I say. "I have major chills."

I step out onto the pavement and walk the walk of the damned.

CHAPTER 69

Later that day I'm checked over by a doctor at the Kingston Medical Center emergency room and given a relatively clean bill of health, if you call numerous lacerations, bruises, sprains, the re-opened cut on my left pinky finger, and yet another slight concussion clean or healthy. Of course, there's nothing that could be done to repair my broken heart.

From the hospital, Crockett and I board a chopper to Albany, where we reconvene over coffee inside a basement interview room that contains a table and some chairs. Crockett's personal laptop is sitting out on the table and it's booted up to a Firefox Google page. Set beside the laptop is the flash drive I handed over to her. It's still protected inside its plastic baggy.

While someone behind the one-way glass films the proceedings, Crockett debriefs me on the events that took place in Florence and how I was able to secure the flash drive from Barter's apartment. When I'm done I ask her the obvious overriding question: Where are Barter and Clyne now?

"In custody of the Italian government. Interpol and the FBI are finally in full cooperative contact. But they are having their turn at the two suspects first before they are extradited to the US."

"And the Russians?"

"Far as we can tell, they're all dead."

"Far as you can tell," I repeat. "There will be more. There always are."

"No word about Iranians, either. No Internet chatter coming from terrorist factions or splinter groups. My guess is Barter and Clyne were about to sell to a private investor."

"What about the flash drive? Anyone think of plugging it into a computer, take a look at the information it holds and why so many people had to die for it, including myself almost a year ago? Including Lola today?"

"You came back to life," Crockett says. "Moonlight rises, remember?"

"Annoying habit of mine. Can't say the same for Lola, can I?"

I stare into the agent's eyes. Eyes I looked into when I made love to her less than a week ago. The emotion I saw in those eyes is now replaced with anxiety.

She picks up the plastic baggy, unzips it, pulls out the flash drive. Her hand trembles slightly when she plugs it into the port. The place goes silent while we wait for the information to appear. Only no information appears. Rather, information shows up, all right, but I'm not entirely sure it's the information the FBI has been expecting. Instead of the locations of rogue nuclear warhead sites, the flash drive stores only a single black-and-white photograph.

I recognize it as the shadow of a man who was seared into a concrete sidewalk when he was suddenly vaporized by the atomic bomb dropped on Hiroshima back in August of 1945.

I've seen the picture many times before. On TV. In school. On the computer. In museums. In back issues of *Time* magazine and *National Geographic*. One of those images you can never quite comprehend, the record of a blast so violent it actually evaporates a human being, leaving only his shadow burned into the pavement.

No matter how many times Crockett plays with the drive, no matter how many times she reinstalls it or reboots her computer, the drive produces only the same thing.

The man's shadowy remains.

I make out the sound of collective laughter coming through the glass.

"Cut the chatter!" Crockett shouts. Then to me. "You said you were sure this was the true flash drive."

I shake my head. "I told you I had *a* flash drive. I had no way of knowing if it was the one you were after. I could only go on what Lola was telling me."

She pulls the flash drive out of the computer, stuffs it into her pants pocket.

"You can go, Moonlight," she says, sounding hollow. "Stay in town for a while until this thing is sorted out. We might need you for additional questioning."

"Sure thing," I say. "No travel plans at present. Only funeral plans."

I head for the door.

"You need a ride," she adds as I place my hand onto the knob, "someone can drive you home."

"Not necessary," I say. "I'll walk. It's not far. 'Sides, I want to stop off for a quick drink, maybe catch some of that special Thursday night Giants game on the NFL Network."

I look at her and I can tell we're both thinking the same thing: Zumbo…the Zump. No doubt the big man is being held inside a holding tank in the Albany County Jail, his career with the feds as dead as his football career. As fucked up and crippled as his knees.

That's when something flashes in my brain like a lightbulb. Tapping my forehead with my fisted hand, I say, "Oh, and I almost forgot. There's that little matter of forgiving my IRS debt to Mrs. Doris E. Walsh's boss."

Crockett casually waves her right hand in the air like she's swatting away a common housefly. "Forgiven," she says. "But no more terroristic letters, OK?"

"Roger that, chief." I open the door. "I'll be seeing you, Crockett."

But she doesn't answer me, because we both know that seeing one another again is an impossibility. She just slaps her laptop closed and sits down hard in her chair. I can't imagine her frustration, but I'm sure it must be profound.

I walk out of the interview room, closing the door gently behind me.

EPILOGUE

Outside the FBI satellite office, I hook a right onto Broadway. Indian summer is officially history. The late fall air has turned cold and crisp, the stars clearly visible in a cloudless night sky. Football weather, my dad used to call it.

I pull a cigarette from the pack in my pocket, fire it up. In the distance, colorful flashing neon announcing "Bar" and "Grill" beckons me to dark, lonely interiors, but I keep walking. I smoke and every so often I choke up at the thought of a lifeless Lola lying on the highway pavement, and the narrow streak of blood that ran down from her left eye and over her lips. I think about how, in the end, the bitter earth can be so cold.

I choke up, but I refuse to shed any more tears for a woman who no longer loved me so much as she loved another. Inevitably, my love for her wasn't enough to save her life.

As I walk deeper into the city, I sense I will never love truly again. Not like I loved her anyway.

Love giveth and love taketh away, and when it's all said and done, we're no further ahead than we were when it all began with a glance and a friendly smile over a backyard picket fence all those years ago. Or maybe I'm wrong. Maybe we're richer for the experience. Or perhaps we're just numb to our own lies and hopeless wishes. Lola's certainly numb.

Lola is dead.

But as the song says, life goes on. All it takes is to move one foot in front of the other. So then, that's what I do. I move one foot in front of the other and I smoke my cigarette, and when I come to the storm sewer grate that eventually empties out into the nearby Hudson River, I reach into my leather coat and pull out the second plastic baggy.

I pull out the second flash drive, hold it in my hand.

Had Lola been aware of the phony flash drive? Had she concocted some kind of silly plan to keep the real one for herself? Did she plan on keeping the drive as a *fuck-you* to the men in her life who had loved her and wronged her? Maybe selling it to the highest bidder on her own so that she could live a life free of worry? Free of Albany and all its ghosts?

No. That wouldn't be like the Lola I once knew and loved.

But then, perhaps that's just wishful thinking.

God works in mysterious ways, so they say. But then, so do the lust for money and the incomprehensible craving for love.

I think of the phony flash drive that produced the picture of that poor man who was vaporized on that sunny day so long ago in Japan. The picture suggests that the flash drive in my possession is the real deal. The fortune maker, and potentially, the mass murderer. But why should I care now that I'm alone and without love? All it would take to sell the thing off is a few well-placed phone calls. I'd cash a big check and, as they say, move on with my life. Somewhere south of the border. Or what the hell, maybe I'd head back to Florence for a while.

In my hand, I support a few ounces of plastic that contain the weight of the world. I drop it to the pavement, crush it with my booted heel, and kick the crushed remnants into the sewer with my boot tip. Pulling the collar up on my leather coat, I light another cigarette and head for the bars.

Alone.

The New York Giants kick off in just ten minutes.

Who knows, this might be our year to finally go all the way.

The End

ABOUT THE AUTHOR

Vincent Zandri is the best-selling author of *The Innocent, Godchild, The Remains, Moonlight Falls, The Concrete Pearl, Scream Catcher, Moonlight Rises,* and the forthcoming *Murder by Moonlight.* He received his MFA in writing from Vermont College, and his work has been translated into several languages. An adventurer, foreign correspondent, and freelance photojournalist for *RT, GlobalSpec,* and *IBTimes,* among others, Zandri lives in New York.